Robert Reid

QUANTUM SHIFT

Global Crisis and Democratic Transformation

The book was printed
digitally on-demand.

© 2014 united p. c. publisher

ISBN 978-3-7103-0666-2
Jacket design, page design and
typesetting: united p. c. publisher

The author is responsible
for the content and correction.

www.united-pc.eu

CONTENTS

INTRODUCTION

Jimmy Reid, in his historic 'Glasgow University, Rectorial Address' in 1972, argued for a 'creative re-orientation of society'. This, he said, would help to 'gear our society to social need, not personal greed', whereby the relations between capital, labour and markets were fundamentally re-arranged to institute an 'enrichment of the whole quality of life', supported by a holistic or ecological world view to benefit all of humanity and the planet. In present circumstances this might take a 'paradigm shift' in our awareness and consciousness. It was T.S. Kuhn who put forward the controversial idea of a paradigm shift that constituted an explanation for the emergence of scientific revolutions. A paradigm is a theoretical framework through which 'normal science' functions. This framework is breached when more and more scientific theories and results begin to contradict the conceptual underpinnings of the old paradigm. When a crisis point is reached, a new paradigm emerges. Copernicus' claim that the Earth circled the sun is a prime example of a classic paradigm shift. Thus the scientific revolution of the 17th Century was, in essence, a qualitative shift from an 'organic' Medieval world view to the Newtonian 'mechanistic' view of the cosmos. This shift cultivated progressive advances in science, culture and society leading ultimately to the profound social transformation we now refer to as 'modernity' or the modern world. More specifically, Newtonian physics epitomised a paradigm shift that emerged from the scientific revolution of the 17th century, through the preparatory genius of Copernicus, Kepler, Galileo, Bacon and Descartes. This predominant scientific shift, greatly influenced the natural and social sciences that followed and eventually created a scientific, secular based cultural transformation which now dominates our beliefs, values, attitudes, social and economic relationships and political decision making.

The main proposition of this book and its relevance to social transformation is the contention that culturally, socially, economically and politically, Western civilisation is locked into an outdated Newtonian-Cartesian, scientific paradigm. This paradigm - in relation to our perceptions of who we are, our values, beliefs, attitudes and behavioural patterns, combined with the secularisation of society and its contemporary materialistic connotations pertaining to the meaning and purpose of human existence - is now, with certain important qualifications, past its sell by date. This judgement does not nullify Newton's scientific achievements or the current value of the Newtonian paradigm and the radical progress it has promoted in science and technology to benefit our health, education and living standards. It is, however, in its mechanistic, materialist world view a limiting paradigm in terms of resolving mankind's contemporary pressing problems. The history of science shows that scientific paradigms go through progressive and retrogressive stages of human development and in the latter phase can act as a theoretical straitjacket to further scientific and social progress thus legitimizing a world view that is taken for granted and defining what is possible and not possible. Mankind is at a stage now where social structures and patterns of behaviour have become rigid and inflexible and unable to adapt creatively to crisis driven situations.

The new paradigm of quantum physics emerged at the turn of the 20th century and has become the most successful, physical and practical scientific theory to date. But for all its critical impact on modern science, digital and social media technology it is little understood in its radical philosophic, social and cultural implications, even by scientists working outside physics. It is in essence a holistic and ecological world view as opposed to the present Newtonian mechanistic and reductionist view of reality. However, the Newtonian paradigm, because of its continuing practical usefulness, still has a powerful hold on our perceptions, consciousness and mindset. The argument presented here is that the revolution in quantum physics is at the heart of another cutting edge cultural and evolutionary transformation as profound as the Newtonian shift in science and consciousness before it. We are now entering a new era where old certainties are crumbling, not just in science but in the fields of the 'social and natural sciences' where new research criteria are now challenging the conceptual framework of the old paradigm that continues to mistake 'the map for the territory'.

PART ONE

1 THE GLOBAL CRISIS

It is becoming more evident by the day that humanity is facing a global crisis of multi-dimensional proportions. It is not only a crisis of late industrial civilisation with its ecological devastation, environmental pollution, resource degradation, social discontent and political alienation. It is a world that has lost any sense of enlightened visionary purpose, dignified human values and ethical or moral standards of conduct; a world of economic, political and media corruption; violence and criminality reflected through contrived wars, terrorist plots, urban riots, global social unrest, human trafficking, religious, sectarian, race and ethnic conflicts, street gang culture and widespread, deeply felt psychological insecurity. While famine, malnutrition and infectious diseases plague the Third World, chronic degenerative and psychological 'diseases of civilisation' have attained the status of 'social pathologies' in the West; heart, cancer and strokes being the main killers while depression, schizophrenia, suicides, obesity, drug abuse and alcoholism all point to behavioural and psychiatric disorders. When combined with obscene levels of wealth, power and material affluence sitting alongside gross economic inequalities, poverty and deprivation, these 'dis-eases' of civilisation appear to predict a future of social and cultural fragmentation, disintegration, and seemingly intractable problems. Is humanity now at a 'tipping point'? According to Ervin Laszlo, "We live in a crucial epoch – an epoch of instability and change... When instability reaches the critical point, the system either collapses or shifts to a new state of dynamic stability. These critical 'tipping points' constitute Macroshifts, which involve all aspects and segments of society: the rich and the poor, the economic and the political systems, the private as well as the public sector." (Ervin Laszlo, Quantum Shift in the Global Brain, 2008, P 17)

Compounding and highlighting this general malaise is the present global banking and financial crisis, the social and economic ramifications of which are yet to fully emerge. This crisis – of which the Euro-Zone is a microcosm of its global severity - reflects the instability of neo-liberal or deregulated capitalism and its ideologically motivated practitioners who have reduced Western Civilisation to a world of the 'cash nexus', mass unemployment and rampant social inequalities, now witnessed in most developed and developing countries. Vested economic interests supported by Western governments over the last three decades have entrenched 'turbo capitalism' as the major economic model pursued by corporate banking and financial elites. Their nefarious casino like practices through which they siphon off Mogul style salaries, bonuses and dividends have been all at the expense of long term, socially beneficial economic development linked to fairer and more equal societies. What is of more serious concern in this seemingly anarchic and chaotic world is the corruption of politics, governments and associated institutions by corporate capitalism. Politics is now a well trodden career option interchangeable with corporate power to the extent that political elites see it profitable to kneel at the feet of high finance and curry favour with 'robber barons' in order to ensure either favourable support for their Party's prospects or secure lucrative employment when they retire . Major political parties, whatever their official proclamations, tend to see the electorate as pawns in the political process to be manipulated and sacrificed in the interests of self, power and privilege. Rather than trusting the people by offering genuine prospects of change to bring about more balanced and just societies, politicians, with honourable exceptions, become an integral part of an elite, centralised establishment which generally focuses on individual or party interest to the detriment of local community participation, finally resulting in political alienation and the undermining of democracy itself.

We now live in highly fragmented societies. The above problems are generally viewed and offered forms of resolution in isolation from the total picture which highlights the complex interdependence and interconnection of the issues involved. The various remedies put forward through government policies are generally informed by vested interests and guided by numerous academic experts and specialist elites whose disciplines are similarly fragmented. However, these problems are but facets of the present overarching global, national and community crises which can best be understood only in relation to a profound transformational, cultural change. Although society now generally recognises the need for the integration of knowledge, interdisciplinary approaches and more holistic solutions to problems, it is still rooted in a limiting conceptual framework, ultimately stemming from the Newtonian mechanistic and reductionist vision of society and culture.

History illustrates that civilisations go through a process of origins, development, disorder, disintegration and renewal. It is from this process, a process Toynbee referred to as 'challenge and response'; in the interaction between the disintegration of the old and the creation of the new a more advanced civilisation arises, attains equilibrium and over time follows the same pattern of breakdown, dissolution and eventual renaissance. This brief , broad and necessarily incomplete introduction to the main premise that Western Civilisation is in the process of radical evolutionary change and ultimately disintegration in its present form is simply the background through which to examine the respective limitations and potential possibilities of the old and new paradigms of science and culture. It is, therefore, necessary to look in some depth at these old and new paradigms to grasp the major influence the old Newtonian paradigm has had and continues to have on Western culture and the potential that the new quantum paradigm has in giving birth to a new global civilisation.

2 THE NEWTONIAN CLOCKWORK UNIVERSE

The Newtonian, Cartesian paradigm grew out of what Tawney in his book, 'Religion and the Rise of Capitalism' referred to as a 'Church Civilisation'. This was a civilisation that, despite its destructive episodes, was by its structure, nature and world view an organic and spiritual universe. It was replaced through a revolution in physics and astronomy by a universe that was conceived as a clockwork machine which has become the major metaphor of our time. Copernicus, Kepler and Galileo changed our view of the universe through empirical, quantifiable and mathematical descriptions of nature. Francis Bacon, whose strong belief in experimentation, changed our view of the scientific quest to that of not simply understanding the natural world but to that of exploiting and dominating it to the point of 'hounding' and 'torturing' her 'secrets from her'. The ancient wisdom of the planet as a 'nurturing mother' disappeared and was replaced by an assertive, patriarchal view of science.

Rene Descartes was driven by a 'vision' and a 'dream' that 'all science is certain, evident knowledge' and we should 'reject all knowledge which is merely probable'. His famous statement, 'I think, therefore I exist' created a separation in his thought between mind and body and its consequential mind, brain relationship. This division between mind and matter has produced an ambivalent effect on the whole of Western thought. Descartes' mathematical methodology is still useful today but only if its limits are recognised. The highly logical Cartesian analytic method has been extremely useful both in scientific research and technological development. Its emphasis, however, on reducing natural phenomena to their constituent parts has left a legacy of academic fragmentation and reductionist methodology that tends to focus on the trees at the expense of the wood, which eventually gave rise to the quantum maxim that the 'whole is more than the sum of the parts'.

It was Descartes' philosophy that laid the foundations and provided the conceptual framework for the view that humankind lived in a material universe governed by mathematical laws. In this mechanical universe, meaning, life and spirituality were excluded and banished from scientific endeavour. Although the presence of God was essential in Descartes' and Newton's thought it was only as a first principle to set the ordered mechanical Universe in motion. With the development of science and technology, the God principle started to wither away. In the years following Descartes, the mechanical Universe became the conceptual basis for a radically new paradigm of science which replaced the previous organic, spiritual view of the Medieval Universe. The organic view of the Universe implied values that were holistic and ecological in their intent and as such placed constraints on behaviour that ran contrary to upholding those beliefs. In this respect, Descartes agreed with Bacon's view that as scientific materialism progressed so the Medieval sanctions were raised and the exploitation and manipulation of nature proceeded apace, thus confirming his view to 'render ourselves the masters and possessors of nature'. (Quoted in The Turning Point, Capra, P46)

In viewing the Universe as a cosmic machine it was only a step to viewing life, plants, animals and humans as sophisticated machines. Descartes affirms this in his statement, 'I consider the human body as a machine...My thought... compares a sick man and an ill made clock with my idea of a healthy man and a well made clock'. (quoted in The Turning Point, Capra P47) Thus the origins of the famous 'Clockwork Universe'. By equating living things to clockwork mechanisms, Descartes has had an overwhelming influence on the life sciences. This clockwork view of looking at living organisms paved the way for great advances in the life sciences, especially in biology and medicine. However, in treating living organisms as mechanisms has encouraged a 'reductionist fallacy' that severely limits other fruitful methods and approaches to knowledge and experimentation. But in spite of these limitations Descartes' methodology and 'clarity of thought remain immensely valuable'. (The Turning Point, P48 Fritjof Capra) Descartes' vision of the Universe and nature as machines provided the conceptual structure through which the life science methodologies were profoundly influenced, followed later by the social sciences, eventually defining the purpose, values, attitudes and meaning of Western Civilisation itself. But in Descartes' life his philosophy remained only a vision. It had to wait for Newton's 'grand synthesis' in an all encompassing mathematical model of the mechanistic Universe to lay a secure foundation upon which Western Science made astounding rational and material progress.

Newton's theory was stated in his 'Mathematical Principles of Natural Philosophy' or 'The Principia' for short. In this work he brought Bacon's empirical, inductive method and Descartes' rational, deductive method together and inspired a methodology which has formed the basis of investigating the natural sciences to the present day. In Newton's model, time and space were absolutes forming no connection with the material world. These dimensions simply allowed material atomic particles to move in accordance with the natural forces of gravity exerted on them. Being a mechanical, clockwork Universe it required God to set the particles, gravitational forces and the laws of motion running, all of which, being governed by exact mathematical laws. This in turn confirmed the deterministic nature of the Newtonian, Cartesian Universe, a mechanical Universe that could be predicted with absolute certainty given sufficient variables and data. Because the physical world was viewed as a gigantic machine, divine inspiration was only required to set it in motion. The material earth was not in itself divine and with the advances in science and technology, inspired by Newton's achievement, God and the divine gradually gave way to the secularisation of mainstream Western society, leaving a growing, spiritual vacuum in its wake. The mechanisation of nature, secularisation and the Cartesian separation of mind and matter led inevitably to the view that the world and the Universe could be analysed and described objectively. With Newton's world view firmly grounded in mathematically proven universal laws, physics became the model for all the natural and life sciences. Descartes put it this way, ' All philosophy is like a tree. The roots are metaphysics, the trunk is physics, and the branches are all the other sciences' (quoted in 'The Turning Point', Capra, P55)

Physics, astronomy, biology, medicine and psychology had been outlined in mechanistic terms in Descartes' visionary thought. After Newton's ground breaking physics, 18th century thinkers began to apply mechanistic principles to the study of human society and human nature. The Age of Enlightenment, was such a flowering of the rational edifice created by Descartes and Newton that some enthusiasts considered 'social physics' an appropriate name for the high minded study of human society. Indeed, the philosopher, John Locke became the principal advocate of applying mechanistic physics to a social and human setting so much so that human beings were described as the fundamental 'building block' of an atomistic society. In following Newtonian, Cartesian reductionist methodology Locke likened the patterns of human behaviour in society to the motion of atoms in the physical world and deduced that such behaviour could be applied to understanding and solving problems in economics and politics. Greatly influenced by the pessimistic philosophy of Thomas Hobbes, Locke adopted his belief that all knowledge was derived from sensory perception thus planting the idea that at birth the mind was a complete blank or 'tabula rasa' as Locke referred to it. This idea went on to play a profound role in the theoretical foundation of behaviourism and psychoanalyses. Locke strongly believed that natural laws if applied to human society would form the basis of freedom, equality and the right to property as the 'fruits of one's labour'. These values from which individualism, property rights, free markets and representative government were derived became the value system of the Enlightenment and the American, 'Declaration of Independence'.

Once set in motion, the Newtonian, Cartesian rationalist approach to scientific endeavour unleashed material progress on a literally, industrial scale. In Newton's own field of physics, the discovery of electro -magnetism replaced the notion of material force with a wave-like force-field and as consequence seriously undermined the mechanistic theory of the universe. The concept of evolution also emerged to further challenge the idea of the mechanistic universe and dethrone the classical and medieval notion of the 'great chain of being' which,in essence, fixed the universe and all natural and human phenomena to their place beneath an omniscient God. The biologist Lamarck turned the idea of the 'chain of being' on its head and contended that all living phenomena evolved from simple forms of life to more complex forms through environmental conditions. Like Newton with physics, Charles Darwin synthesized the work of Lamarck and others before him and established the concept of evolution as the new biological reality. Physics and evolutionary biology fed off one another but came to different conclusions regarding the nature of reality. The biologists found that evolutionary life forms progressed from simple to more ordered complex forms while in physics, evolutionary movement went towards increasing disorder and entropy. Although Maxwell's electrodynamics and Darwin's theory of evolution unquestionably undermined the Newtonian, mechanistic world view its application to many physical processes and procedures was still valid and true in relation to its appropriate context. It was not until the advent of Einstein's relativity theory and quantum theory that the mechanistic universe suffered a theoretical demise that it could not recover from, apart from what has already been said about its continuing practical, day to day usefulness. In this respect it is worth remembering that, " The reductionist description of organisms can therefore be useful and may in some cases be necessary. It is dangerous only when it is taken to be the complete explanation. Reductionism and holism, analysis and synthesis, are complementary approaches that, used in proper balance, help us obtain a deeper knowledge of life." (The Turning Point, F. Capra, 1982, P288)

3 THE MECHANISTIC WORLD VIEW

Before looking at Quantum theory and its impact on the modern world it is important to acknowledge the profound influence the mechanistic world view still has on our society and culture. It is not a question of how wrong Newtonian physics is or how right Quantum theory is. All science is an approximation until it is replaced by other improved approximations. Quantum physics - theoretically,technologically and philosophically - has gone far beyond Newtonian science. The latter, however, still influences Western thought to such a degree that the social, political, economic, biological and medical sciences - whose research and practice were not only originally stimulated by this paradigm - have basked, ever since in the relative success of its major by product, 'scientific materialism'. "The sheer power and simplicity of Newton's three mechanical laws of motion, and the apparent force of the new empirical method, drew nearly every influential social, political and economic thinker of the seventeenth, eighteenth and nineteenth centuries to use them as a model."(The Quantum Society, Mind, Physics and a New Social Vision, P.3, Danah Zohar and Ian Marshall)

Western culture's social, economic and political assumptions of 'modernity' are firmly rooted in mechanistic perceptions of reality which are daily reinforced by the technology and metaphorical imagery that surrounds us. Evidence of Newton's ubiquitous influence is verified in the work of Thomas Hobbes, John Locke, Adam Smith, Karl Marx, Charles Darwin, Freud and August Comte who not only created the term 'sociology' but first called the discipline 'social physics'. These, and other thinkers of the Enlightenment and industrial age, are the very pillars of the generally agreed wisdom upon which the whole scientific edifice of Western Civilisation stands. They were all men and women of their time who contributed inestimable value to securing the Newtonian paradigm as the established world view of 'scientific materialism' and, in the process, catapulted Western society into the modern, 'democratic' age. Although Newton's Universe had God as the first mover of the cosmos, later developments in the sciences he had unleashed gradually eliminated this omnipotent power from his equations of natural law. It was believed that the deterministic precision of Newtonian physics, especially the idea of the clockwork mechanism, could be applied to the state, economics, politics, government and ultimately human beings, now viewed as 'living machines'. Metaphors abound in our language which express a mindset still firmly attached to Newtonian mechanistic ways of thinking. "… expressions like 'the wheels of government' and the 'machinery of state' and in the philosophical implications of artificial intelligence – we are 'mind machines',we 'switch on' and 'switch off', we 'blow our fuses' and are 'programmed' for success or failure".

(The Quantum Society, Mind, Physics and a New Social Vision, P4, Danah Zohar and Ian Marshall)

It should be stressed that it is not only 20th century writers who offer a critique of the Newtonian mechanistic world view. William Blake along with many Romantic poets and artists foretold of the social impact of this model of reality. Newton's mechanistic thinking was seen by Blake as 'single vision and Newton's sleep', a view which is depicted in his famous painting of Newton 'measuring the ratio'. Blake's critique of Bacon, Locke and Newton's empiricism was based on their reduction of nature and human nature and their common, symbiotic relationships to oversimplified mechanistic measurements which he branded as false reasoning, and which he believed was one of the 'spectre's' haunting humanity's evolutionary development towards a more 'spiritual' vision.

The !8th century Enlightenment espoused the values of individualism, reason, human progress and a belief in mechanistic science. It was from this science and the rational belief in human progress that modern Western economies evolved and drew their strength. The idea of progress legitimized the exploitation of natural resources, and with that, the hijacking of whole continents and the conquest of indigenous cultures and peoples that inhabited them. The Romantic movement by contrast rejected the mechanistic imagery of Newtonian science and celebrated a living, organic world portrayed in art, song and poetry. This produced a long lasting division between town and country and a very personal and private adherence to a living, animate, organic landscape as opposed to a dead mechanistic professional belief system as practised in the physical, social, economic, political and biological sciences. Technological advances such as TV eventually brought this animate and organic world to life in contradiction to the official scientific assumptions held by the 'hard sciences'. The above is evidence of a growing alienation of man from nature, a precursor to the increasing alienation of man from man and man from himself.

4 ALIENATION: A MALAISE OF THE WESTERN SPIRIT

The Newtonian mechanistic universe had a prime influence on the development and establishment of all academic disciplines, including those of the social sciences. The social sciences, in particular, wished to emulate the precision of Newtonian science and so raise their status and authority to that of the physical sciences. The impact of the Newtonian paradigm on industrial and technological expansion and on academic disciplines inadvertently helped to create the long term cultural conditions for mass alienation which has left a devastating and enduring effect on the functioning of Western society. As already stated, the Newtonian paradigm was appropriate for the historical time in which it came to the fore. Newtonian science, combined with the 18th century Enlightenment, prepared the way for the emergence of the 'Age of Revolutions' – the American, French and Industrial revolutions - and the subsequent political freedoms associated with liberal 'bourgeois' democracy, so necessary in the promotion and pursuit of economic and individualistic self-interest compatible with the rise of a thriving capitalist economy and its driving entrepreneurial class. These circumstances, – metaphorically likened to Locke's impenetrable atoms or billiard balls colliding and bouncing off one another - produced human behavioural patterns of conduct which Thomas Hobbes in the Leviathan viewed as a 'war of every man against every man'. In political terms, this mindset was about, "Finding some way to balance all the conflicting interests that result in a society" and " has been the basis for adversarial democracy and the familiar confrontational style of modern political parties." (The Quantum Society: Mind, Physics and a New Social Vision: Danah Zohar & IanMarshall, 1993 P. 4)

Newton's 'clockwork' representation of the universe reinforced the alienation and separation of man from man and man from nature. In a mechanistic world, nature becomes an alien force to be exploited and conquered, leading inexorably to the present ecological crisis. Mechanism, when applied to human behaviour, institutionalises attitudes of certainty over ambiguity, rigidity over flexibility, predictability over changeability and hierarchy over grass roots democracy. These and many other examples of conflicting opposites in our society are not the opposites of Daoist paradox which reconcile and reveal essential truths about a culture. They are grounded in bitter egotistical power struggles and intransigent bureaucracy, the latter being one of the major offshoots of the mechanistic society, reinforcing hierarchical power structures, euphemistically viewed as 'ladders of ascending and descending authority.' Taking Hobbes comment of 'war of every man...' literally, nation states steeped in this mindset descend into confrontation and ultimate military conflict which was everywhere prevalent in his world and which has continued for three hundred years of imperial, colonial and world wars into the 20th C. and beyond to localised conflicts in the 21st C.

The much criticised and socially labelled 'expert' is a contemporary product of a society that revels in reductive mechanistic approaches to solving problems. This person is required to be highly knowledgeable in a particular area of expertise, objective and upholding of a value free detachment from any subjective bias. But in reducing knowledge and information to fragments he becomes more and more divorced from the whole picture which this methodology inevitably conceals. Reductionism leads to fragmentation and alienation which, in terms of human cost, can, in its extreme form, be expressed in degrees of mental illness, a health issue which places one in four persons in Britain in this category during a lifetime, to say nothing about the number of suicides, especially among the young. Mechanistic psychiatry is the dominant approach to treating mental illness in that one of the major assumptions regarding this illness stems from what is believed to be a bio-chemical imbalance in the material brain which can only be controlled by chemical drugs. The symptoms may be controlled but usually at the expense of the client's precarious psycho-physical state, while the multi-faceted causes go ignored. The reason for this being, that "Rigid adherence to the Newtonian-Cartesian paradigm has had particularly detrimental consequences for the practice of psychiatry and psychotherapy. It is largely responsible for the inappropriate application of the medical model to areas of psychiatry that deal with problems of living, rather than diseases." (Beyond The Brain; Stanislav Grof, 1985, P25)

The 'problems of living' observation is probably one of the more likely explanations for the recurrent school and other mass murders in America rather than simply focusing on isolated, disturbed individuals. These individuals are by any standard alienated, either from themselves, their family or from a society that seeks refuge from its own national obsession with insecurity in literally, defending to the death its gun culture and status as the world's policeman. With 95,000 deaths in one year from guns it is clearly evident that these deaths are the outcome of an inflexible, dogmatic interpretation of the American Constitution which gives gun culture its apparent legitimacy. Since its inception, the American psyche and society has always been seen as a conquering nation, first to expel the British, then overcome with military superiority the continent's indigenous tribes and afterwards, the establishment of an industrial society through civil war. As American capitalism developed into imperialism and 'manifest destiny' it looked beyond its borders for economic expansion and the further pursuit of international security, which always happened to be in the interests of American big business. The emergence of agencies like the CIA and a powerful military-industrial complex – which now appropriates half the American budget - is the culmination of the United States efforts to secure America, both internally and externally, from a world perceived to be either for it or against it, with all the political and economic consequences that flow from that. This may be a long way from the slaying of school children by disturbed individuals. In the end, it goes back to the American Constitution which has been mechanistically reduced from a different time, place and purpose and applied to the present without acknowledging the history of the intervening years and thus an appreciation of the whole phenomenon through which these individual mass killings could be better understood.

Alienation has nowhere been revealed so starkly than in the industrial and corporate manufacturing sector of the capitalist economy. The organisation of mass production has in its mechanistic functions reduced human beings to 'factors of production' and 'units of consumption' who become ultimately alienated from themselves, each other and as Marx said, 'the products of their own labour.' Charlie Chaplin's film on the machine society exemplifies the robotic nature of modern production methods which the car industry amply demonstrates. Nowhere in the modern world, apart from politics, exhibits the proverbial 'dog eat dog' mentality more than the global corporation, which, in its behavioural characteristics, has been likened to being 'psychopathic' in its cut-throat ruthlessness and greed for profit and expansion. Is it an exaggeration to claim that alienation has become the major social disease of Western culture and with it a deep suspicion of, and absence of trust in all the political institutions of representative government, the legal justice system, policing and security services, mass media, finance, banking and transnational corporations? All these institutions have become associated with one form of corruption or another and collectively are increasingly undermining what is left of participatory democracy itself.

Alienation, however, is most marked in its dehumanising effect on working people, the unemployed and those suffering deprivation. It is ironic that at a time when major cities were burning in England a Foundation in memory of Jimmy Reid was being established in Scotland. If one word could describe the underlying expression of this conflagration it would be 'alienation', the very theme of of Jimmy Reid's Rectorial Address to the students of Glasgow University in 1972. Jimmy Reid provided the classic description of alienation. He defined it as the "cry of men who feel themselves the victims of blind economic forces beyond their control." It was "the frustration of ordinary people excluded from the processes of decision making." It was, "the feeling of despair and hopelessness." He was aware that alienation also manifested itself in rapacious attitudes and dehumanising behaviour and in this respect he was not simply referring to criminal anti-social conduct but to the insensitivity, ruthlessness and immorality of those who exert power and influence over their fellow men and women.

To Jimmy Reid this waste was a 'social crime' on an industrial scale and as such society was the loser and everyone a victim. However, when it came to the fundamental cause of alienation and the distorted human values that were the products of it, he highlighted the economic ascendency of transnational corporations, the profit motive driving the "centralisation and concentration of power in fewer and fewer hands" and the subservience of governments to their needs, all to the detriment of moral and ethical behaviour and the 'negation of democracy.' Although he wrote the following indictment in 1972 he could well have been describing the power of the neo-liberal state; "Profit is the sole criterion used by the establishment to evaluate economic activity. From the rat race to lame ducks....It's more reminiscent of a human menagerie than human society. The power structures that have inevitably emerged from this approach threaten and undermine our hard-won democratic rights. Giant monopoly companies and consortia dominate almost every branch of our economy. The men who wield effective control within these giants exercise a power over their fellow men which is frightening and is a negation of democracy." (The Glasgow Rectorial Address, April 1972, Jimmy Reid) Where is it possible to find a critique so damning of a reductive, mechanistic approach to an economy which purports to distribute fairness and justice to all its citizens?

Alienation in its industrial, technological and social dimensions highlights the human condition of modern society, given the global ascendancy of neo-liberal, corporate states. Even conservative governments sense the creeping malaise of alienation -

often interpreted as apathy - through the loss of community and the 'happiness deficit' that goes with it at its core. Unfettered capitalism and the increasing inequality, corruption and nihilism it has created has reached a point where it can no longer even pretend to serve people, in theory or in practice. Neo-liberal capitalism is a mechanistic monolith created from mathematical formulae, quantification, measurement, 'commodification' and reductionist principles which bear no relationship to the economic reality real people face in their daily lives. However, real people had to face the way in which Milton Friedman and his 'Chicago Boys' inflicted their fundamentalist theory on the world through terror, torture and murder in Latin America and ideologues from right-wing think tanks and politicians in the West, whose credo is privatisation, deregulation, public spending cuts and brazen attacks on welfare states.

5 THE ECONOMICS OF INJUSTICE

When Bill Clinton coined the phrase, 'its the economy stupid' he was simply emphasising what all Western Governments depend upon to maintain their political power - delivering higher standards of living, ever climbing consumption and productive employment. So focused have Western Governments become in satisfying consumer demands and high employment through economic growth that their very dependence for political survival in the 21st century rests wholly on the now stuttering engine of neo-liberal capitalism. This dependence in turn has placed democratic governments and its institutions at the mercy of international finance, banking and transnational corporations. According to David Harvey, "Neoliberal theorists are...profoundly suspicious of democracy....Neoliberals therefore tend to favour governance by experts and elites. A strong preference exists for government by executive order and by judicial decision rather than democratic and parliamentary decision making. Neoliberals prefer to insulate key institutions, such as the Central Bank, from democratic pressure." (A brief History of Neoliberalism: David Harvey, 2005, P66.)

The Western economy – indeed the world economy – is locked into the philosophy of economic expansion and consumption. This on a planet whose resources are finite and according to the latest scientific research is fast approaching a 'tipping point' to ecological 'armageddon'. John Stuart Mill predicted this outcome long before it entered the awareness of the political or public domains; " If the earth must lose that great pleasantness which it owes to things that the unlimited increase of wealth and population would extirpate from it....I sincerely hope, for the sake of posterity, that they will be content to be stationary, long before necessity compels them to it". (Quoted in Farewell to Growth: Serge Latouche, 2007, P1) The Enlightenment, being the age of reason, stimulated what has become an irrational, obsession with technological progress through unlimited economic growth. Primarily based on Newtonian materialism, linear thinking and the Baconian belief that nature be mastered and dominated for human purposes gave the driving forces of embryonic, industrial capitalism the legitimacy to exploit and plunder the earth for the benefit of national prestige, colonialism and empire.

In theory, Marx's critique of capitalism and the rise of communist states originally offered an alternative social vision to capitalism. In time, this vision degenerated to being as obsessed with material acquisition, hard technology and centralised bureaucracy as any corporate, capitalist state. Unlimited economic growth, to use Marx's religious metaphor, has become the 'opium of the people', the governments and corporations that relentlessly pursue it and the consumer who has become addicted to it for work, consumption, pleasure and entertainment. The price to be paid for such growth, especially under the global reach of neo-liberalism is severe social consequences, the third world and women in general paying the highest price. The fragmentation and emasculation of labour movements, flexible labour markets, short term contract work and perpetual job insecurity has undermined a traditional sense of dignity, pride in a work ethic and individual self-esteem. Neo-liberal capitalism confirms the role of labour as the proverbial cog in the wheel and therefore expendable in relation to corporate decisions regarding the movement of capital and companies to more lucrative pastures. And all this, influenced by the role of dice in casinos, euphemistically called financial centres. David Harvey sums up the prize for the survivors of the capitalist, machine-like, consumer culture. "Unfortunately, this culture, however spectacular, glamorous, and beguiling perpetually plays with desires without ever conferring satisfactions beyond the limited identity of the shopping mall and the anxieties of status by way of good looks (in the case of women) or of material possessions. 'I shop therefore I am' and possessive individualism together construct a world of pseudo-satisfactions that is superficially exciting but hollow to its core." (A Brief History of Neoliberalism: David Harvey, 2005, P170.) Again, the evidence everywhere points to the social and economic consequences of extreme reductionism, that when applied in a mechanistic way without reference to its impact on the whole of society either ends up in a materialistic culture that has lost all meaning or alternatively like the urban riots in England that could only provide meaning for the participants through the pillaging of material goods and damage to private property.

According to Westminster Government spokesmen on the recent urban riots, the metaphorical 'rats' referred to in Jimmy Reid's rectorial address were now transmuted into 'feral rats' inhabiting a 'feral underclass' scurrying about raiding the consumer larders of the major cities in England. The riots and looting were indeed lawless acts of mindless violence and rampaging criminal behaviour but can they be compared with the equally unlawful but considered acts of deliberate deception by those involved in telephone hacking, police collusion and robbing the public expenses purse or the insatiable greed of a 'feral elite' who brought the world's financial institutions crashing down? At the very least the latter had education and status on their side and fully understood the immoral and unethical dimensions of what they were doing. They represented the institutional pillars of our 'democracy'. Their conduct undermined its very foundations.

The West's contemporary, materialist obsession with undifferentiated growth and the values underpinning it arose deep within the Newtonian mechanistic paradigm. Newton and Descartes were men of their time whose visions necessitated the intervention of a prime mover to set the universe in motion. Some of their beliefs and values, which in Newton's case were entwined in religion and the occult, were later distorted for the sake of expediency and pragmatism. Sir William Petty and John Locke made significant contributions to the evolution of economic thought. However, it was left to Adam Smith's 'Wealth Of Nations' to lay its secure foundation. He espoused the principal of the 'Invisible

Hand' of the market, whereby the self-interest of entrepreneurs would ultimately balance relations between supply and demand and deliver material wealth in support of social 'betterment' for the whole of society. In doing this, Smith contributed to the notion that the absence of human intervention would harmonise economic activity and bring scientific objectivity to the rising discipline of political economy as it was then known.

Smith's economic theory reflected Newton's laws of motion and ideas of equilibrium. It was based on small scale production and assumed a competitive landscape where every entrepreneur competed on an equal footing. Whatever its merits in advancing economics as an 'objective science', Smith's ideas were essentially of theoretical value whose idealism was exposed with the rise of corporate and monopoly capitalism. However, despite the nature of 'petty bourgeois' capitalism from which Smith formulated his economic theory many of today's economists have transformed Smith's idealistic assumptions into hard fact and ignored Mill's prediction that when soil and resources decline so will economic progress. Economics as an academic discipline evolved from the concept of political economy which attempted to integrate economics into a wider social, political and ecological fabric. Today, economics has been reduced to fragmentary analyses of micro and macro mathematical models abstracted from politics and the ethical and moral dimensions which that connection would bestow on its practice. Broad thinking academics like Max Weber, Kenneth Galbraith, Robert Heilbroner, Kenneth Boulding and Hazel Henderson who criticised this reductionist trend have ended up being associated with other disciplines in addition to economics.

The dynamic nature of a rapidly changing society demands that economic theory continuously evolves and adapts to deal with contemporary situations. The discipline's assertion that it is 'value free' and therefore more scientific conceals an underlying value system which is open to the criticism that it is ideologically constrained and because of that, less scientific. Being a discipline that is defined by its focus on the production, distribution and exchange of wealth it is - especially in a predominantly capitalist society forever suffering from cyclical phases of 'boom and bust' – even more value dependent than any of the other social sciences. This value dependency is expressed by Schumacher in theoretically comparing the values behind a materialist capitalist system and a Buddhist economy; in the former the standard of living is measured by maximum consumption and optimal production while the latter focuses on achieving the maximum quality of human well being and optimal consumption.

The consequences of denying or disguising the hidden values embedded in any capitalist economic analysis is to avoid dealing with the real social and political issues confronting the whole society. This avoidance leads to treating economic problems as merely technical and managerial. This technocratic approach appears to be shared by Paul Krugman – a Nobel prize winner - whose critique of the 2008 'credit crunch' is particularly damning: - "... the problem isn't with the economic engine, which is as powerful as ever. Instead, we're talking about what is basically a technical problem, a problem of organisation and coordination – a 'colossal muddle,' - as Keynes put it. Solve this technical problem, and the economy will roar back to life." (End This Depression Now, Paul Krugman, 2012, P 22) Here there is no fundamental critique of the neo-liberal 'engine' itself. Simply apply a few technical tweaks and the motor will spring back to life. The assumption being made is that capitalism is here to stay and by its very nature defies the brightest minds to imagine anything different. According to Krugman, all that the present crisis requires is 'intellectual clarity and political will to act.' He sums it up in a heading, 'Its All about Demand.' And Krugman is not alone. If any academic discipline shows the influence of a Newtonian mechanistic approach to solving economic problems more it is the economics profession, which, in the current crisis, has been generally criticised for its narrow, fragmented, quantitative reductionism. In desperately trying to uphold its 'scientific' credentials through reductionist and quantitative techniques, contemporary economists ignore the qualitative, value laden distinctions so necessary to understanding economic problems in their social, ecological and psychological dimensions.

The employment of abstract quantitative economic models when applied to the profound structural changes brought about by globalisation has created a wide gulf between theory and economic reality. This has led to a deep conceptual crisis within the economics fraternity which has been recognised by both economists themselves and other disciplines. The gap between theory and reality has been highlighted by the present global crisis whereby the application of highly sophisticated mathematical models to real financial and banking problems triggered an economic collapse the world has not seen before. Economic theory has over the last thirty or more years been heavily influenced by the 'Chicago School', a University of Chicago clique of prominent 'idealistic' economists who dreamt of creating the ideal capitalist economy and society and fundamentally change economic thinking. Milton Friedman, the guru of this transformation regarded the capitalist economy as distorted and would require 'bitter medicine' to resolve its flaws. Economic factors, such as supply, demand, inflation and unemployment were envisaged in a radical free-market to be in complete equilibrium and as self-regulating as a natural ecosystem. In conception, it almost surpasses in precision the way in which the Soviet command economy was theoretically supposed to work. Neo-liberalism was indeed portrayed as an exact science, a virtual capitalist Eden on earth, all conforming to a Newtonian mechanistic harmony and reviewed by the Harvard sociologist Daniel Bell as 'a jewelled set of movements' or a 'celestial clock....a work of art'. Unfortunately, the theory was unable to be tested immediately in the real world whence the 'Chicago Boys' developed elaborate mathematical equations and models until the time was ripe for the theory's political ascension.

In time, Friedman's theory found the ideal political leaders who would carry out its fundamentalist tenets. They included,

"U.S. Presidents, British Prime Ministers, Russian oligarchs, Polish finance ministers, Third World dictators, Chinese Communist Party secretaries, International Monetary Fund directors and the past three chiefs of the U.S. Federal Reserve." (The Shock Doctrine, Naomi Klein, P7) The theory was also used in the service of American imperialism in Chile where an elected socialist government was brutally overthrown. Chicago economists, including Friedman himself, advised the Pinochet junta on establishing an unfettered free-market enterprise state. In time, the theory was instrumental in establishing, with CIA support, free-market, tyrannical dictatorships in Chile, Brazil, Uruguay and Argentina. Flying the free-market banner of privatisation, deregulation and social spending cuts - the holy trinity of neo-liberal capitalism - the system would eventually "be imposed in dozens of other countries under the cover of a wide range of crises. But Chile was the counter revolution's genesis – a genesis of terror " (The Shock Doctrine: Naomi Klein, P 95) The dominant theory in the economics firmament now straddled the globe like an ideological colossus, the policies of which have continued to reign despite the 'bitter medicine' it has imposed on the world before and since the 2008 financial and banking crash. From a theory that attempted to eliminate the distortions in the capitalist system through creating the ideal free-market economy, it ironically, in practice has inflicted serious damage on middle income groups and increased poverty and deprivation to lower classes. In effect, neo-liberalism has delivered a world of gross inequalities, mass global unemployment, institutionalised greed and corruption, public alienation and ecological disasters to say nothing of the economic and military intervention and destruction it has spread in the third world and the middle East.

According to Naomi Klein, Friedman regarded social and economic crises as a prime opportunity to inflict unfettered market forces on local communities. This happened in New Orleans when hurricane Katrina hit and in Chile when the Pinochet Junta, supported and guided by the CIA, established a tyrannical

dictatorship on the people. It was from socio-economic trage-
dies like this across the world that she recorded and gave the
sub- title to her book, 'The Rise of Disaster Capitalism'. From
the Falklands War, which gave Mrs Thatcher the 'nationalist ex-
citement' and dominance to attack and fatally weaken the min-
ers strike and with it the trade union movement, she capitalised
on her political advantage and began a frenzy of privatisation
in line with Friedman's and Hayek's economic strategy. The Ar-
gentinian Junta's despotic rule, the debt ridden crisis in Africa and Latin America, the financial crisis in Asia in 1997-98,
China and Russia in the eighties and nineties, America after
9/11 and Iraq's contract, corporate structure were all viewed
by those influenced by the 'Chicago Boys' as 'opportunities' to
exploit these crises conditions and establish the hegemony of
global neo-liberal capitalism. The 2008 crisis has in the process
exposed 'disaster capitalism' as a contemporary breeding ground
for authoritarianism, social and economic tribalism and right
wing extremism bordering on fascism.

Friedman was an idealist whose intentions were to bring,
'truth', 'beauty' and 'hard science' to the world of economics
and ultimately 'freedom' to society. Instead, 'the Chicago Boys',
evolved a theory through which global economic deregulation
both stimulated and consolidated the unlimited pursuit of material wealth, economic growth and consumerism as the quintes-
sential measure of the good society. In practice, the individualistic values, survival of the fittest attitudes and collective mindset
flowing from these materialistic aspirations have brought the
world closer to its social and ecological tipping point. A retired
American Colonel once remarked that, Al Capone operated in
three Chicago city districts while he boasted that he was a 'mus-
cle man for capitalism' who operated on three continents. It
might be said that the 'The Chicago School' and the influence
of its unfettered free-market creed superseded both Al Capone
and the Colonel in globally institutionalising greed and excessive power, exercised far beyond political and democratic control as the highest form of 'possessive individualism' that a fi-

nancial elite anywhere could aspire to. What the 'Chicago Boys' share in spirit with Al Capone and the Colonel – most certainly in Latin America - is the gangsters and military use of terror, torture, murder and intimidation, and in the West, an elite's arrogance of power and a deep distaste for genuine democracy and grass roots participation in decisions that affect people's lives.

The Chicago Boys earnestly believed in their purist economic theory but their economic schooling and grooming of Latin American economists paved the way for more indigenous military dictatorships to emerge. The 'democratic' structures in the West encountered similar 'shock treatment'. The Reagans and Thatchers of the world – all paid up ideologues - had to take account of the economic conditions of the time and their electorates and apply more subtle applications of the theory. In Thatcher's case, she seduced council house occupants into purchasing their homes and so become part of the 'ownership society' while rents soared. The 'shock doctrine' became fully operational when Thatcher took Britain to war with Argentina over the Falklands. Triumphal in her Churchillian stand she was then able to enact the three principals of Friedman's holy trinity, privatisation, deregulation and social welfare cuts. These Latin American regimes and right wing politicians across the world blatantly used Friedman's 'shock doctrine' to give an air of science and logic to policies which their ruling elites and political parties regarded as a godsend in pursuit of counter-revolutionary changes that would establish and secure their long-term financial interests, irrespective of who came to power, conservative parties or labour and liberal social democratic parties.

Neo-liberalism is the epitome of a pristine laissez-faire Capitalism. Unfortunately, by regressing back to a 19th century economic ground zero to usher in 'freedom', 'truth' and 'beauty' has only demonstrated that these values were never compatible with 'unfettered capitalism' nor in solving the pressing problems of climate change, sustainable economic growth and excessive consumerism. If Neo-liberal capitalism illustrates anything it is the dogmatic defence of a fundamentalist creed imposed by right-wing economists with the aid of global corporations, capitalist state structures and compliant politicians. In mechanistically reducing economic and social policy to rigid applications of dogma in the name of science is a travesty of both science and economics. The social sciences in mimicking Newtonian science through placing their emphasis on becoming 'hard sciences' and applying reductionism as their primary methodological approach to knowledge is deeply flawed. It is not the approach that is misguided but the misinterpretation of the method - that the parts explain the whole. The paradigm which we are about to look at argues the opposite; that the whole is greater than the sum of the parts. This implies that a holistic and ecological world view opens the way to a deeper understanding and integration of information and knowledge and is more compatible with the paradigm of quantum physics. However, before looking at the theoretical implications and practical applications of the new paradigm it is worth drawing a general picture regarding the impact of quantum science and its various effects on society as a whole.

PART TWO

6 THE QUANTUM UNIVERSE

Einstein's theories of special and general relativity were revolutionary in that they challenged the Newtonian concepts of space, time and gravity. His monumental life's work to unify electro- dynamics and mechanics was based on his belief that there was a unified harmony within nature. It was, however, the investigation into the atomic and sub-atomic world of matter that not only shattered the mechanistic world view for good but in the process astounded the group of physicists whose classical ways of thinking, language and concepts were no longer appropriate to describe what they had discovered. This sense of amazement is conveyed by Werner Heisenberg, one of the physicist's involved:-"I remember discussions with Bohr which went through many hours till very late at night and ended almost in despair; I went alone for a walk... I repeated to myself again and again the question: Can Nature possibly be so absurd as it seemed to us in these atomic experiments." (quoted in The Turning Point', Capra P. 64/65) The reason why Heisenberg, Bohr and the other quantum physicists questioned the seeming absurdity of sub-atomic reality was the paradoxes it threw up in their experiments. Nature at the sub-atomic level did not respond to classical mechanistic concepts and reductionist approaches in describing the world of space, time, matter, cause and effect, so much so, that even Einstein felt, "as if the ground had been pulled out from under one, with no firm foundation to be seen anywhere, upon which one could have built."(quoted in The Turning Point, Capra, P. 66) So astonishing are the paradoxical revelations of quantum physics and the radical world view that is now emerging, that not all physicists and scientists share in its implied philosophical implications. These implications, concluded from hard experimentation, completely challenged the foundation of a mechanistic universe and replaced it with a holistic, ecological and organic world view. They reveal a dynamic, interconnected reality where wholeness, pattern and process make up an indivisible oneness, a oneness that paradoxically coincides and runs parallel with the visions of the great mystical traditions of the East. (Frijof Capra, The Tao of Physics: An exploration of the parallels between modern physics and Eastern mysticism, 1976)

The most significant discovery is that matter in its atomic and sub-atomic aspect is not solid in the classical 'billiard ball' Newtonian sense. These particles have a paradoxical dual existence in that they are both 'waves' and 'particles' which are continuously interchangeable depending on their situation. This interchangeable duality between particles creates a process or pattern of behaviour where to be precise about one state produces uncertainty in the other state, hence Heisenberg's famous 'uncertainty principle'. The paradoxical nature of the atomic world gave rise to Neil Bohr's equally important 'complementarity' concept that integrated the 'wave-particle duality' to describe the same fundamental reality. Again, this concept of complementarity is integral to the ancient Chinese philosophy of Daoism. The symbols of yin and yang opposites complement the tension within and between each but held together within an inherent wholeness. Matter at the sub-atomic level shows only 'tendencies to exist' not with certainty in specific places and times. These tendencies have only a 'probability' to exist and cannot be equated to sound or water waves. The insubstantial nature of matter swept the proverbial carpet from under the Newtonian belief in its solidity. Material objects transmute into 'patterns of probability' and particles exist not as isolated entities but simply as abstractions, interconnecting and interacting with other illusive entities. This confirms that the material world does not spring from building block units of matter but from what Capra refers to as "a complicated web of relations between the various parts of a unified whole". (The Turning Point, Capra P. 70) This understanding of the universe as a set of relationships and not objects has radical implications for how we relate to the world in general and science in particular.

The sub-atomic phenomena known by physicists as 'non-local' connections go far beyond the idea of Newtonian 'local variables'. Quantum non-local connections demonstrate an instantaneous interaction, whatever the distance, with the whole universe. It was due to this phenomena and the strange nature of probability, that Einstein himself found difficult to accept and was the source of his famous comment that, 'God does not play dice' with the universe. He did, however, accept that Bohr's and Heisenberg's interpretation of quantum theory was consistent but believed that a deterministic interpretation would be found involving local variables. Taking this view showed that Einstein's belief with regard to local variables, despite his revolutionary contribution to undermining the Newtonian mechanistic universe and establishing one of the foundations of quantum physics, was still partially locked into a Cartesian view of the world. The notion of instantaneous non-local connections over vast distances questioned the Newtonian, Cartesian principle of cause and effect and has deep implications for science in general. Quantum theory does not allow for reducing nature to analysable parts and seeking deterministic causal links and laws. Due to the constant interaction between particles there can be no causal links in the classic Newtonian sense and therefore no predictability about when and how events happen. Probability is the only thing that can be predicted. Although sub-atomic behaviour is not arbitrary, it is non-local causes interacting dynamically with the whole that determines the probability of events at this level of matter. As Capra comments:- "Where in classical mechanics the properties and behavior of the parts determine those of the whole, the situation is reversed in quantum mechanics: it is the whole that determines the behavior of the parts." (The Turning Point, Capra, P. 76)

One of David Bohm's many original contributions to Quantum theory was the suggestion that there were close analogies between thought processes and quantum processes. This further added to what James Jeans had said in a much earlier remark that: - "Today there is a wide measure of agreement... that the stream of knowledge is heading towards a non-mechanical reality; the universe begins to look more like a great thought than a great machine." (James Jeans, Quoted in The Turning Point, P. 76) The idea that the processes involved in the interaction between mind and matter should not be surprising in that quantum experiments demonstrated that human consciousness played a key role in determining the observed outcome of these experiments. Mechanistic philosophy would in theory see an electron or any object, for example, as an objective entity while the evidence from quantum experiments showed that mind or consciousness at this level has a profound influence on the outcome. These experiments, demonstrate no distinction between the observer and the observed thus completely undermining the Cartesian separation of mind and matter. Quantum revelations have significant implications for society in general and science in particular. Quantum reality invalidates objective descriptions of natural phenomena and questions the ideal classical belief in science being value free. Accordingly, the observation of natural phenomena cannot be separated from the conscious minds of the observers; that is, the results and their applications are conditioned by the observers value system and thought patterns, whether they are aware of it or not. The implication of this is that scientists are ethically and morally responsible for the nature of their research, especially of that involved in physics, through which it can lead, negatively or positively, in the direction of 'the Bomb or the Buddha.'

If consciousness plays a critical role in the observation of matter, so does its dynamic, interactive nature. Matter at the sub-atomic level is forever active and restless, especially when confined within molecules, atoms and particles where vibrational velocities reach phenomenal speeds. At these 'light' speeds, relativity and quantum theory are both required to explain such activity. The conclusion here is that there is nothing static in nature. Everything is in a state of flux and moves in an interactive, interdependent way and provides forms of stability through the dynamic balance of the whole. Quantum and relativity theory run contrary to any common sense Newtonian conception of solidity which has to be abandoned when matter or mass is conceived to be what Einstein mathematically formulated in his famous equation as E=mc2; in plain language, energy =mass. The newly discovered Higgs Boson particle, commonly referred to as 'the God Particle' is apparently the 'glue' that helps to create mass. In this context, time and space become a 'four-dimensional continuum' which reveals a world where sub-atomic particles interact to create dynamic patterns of energy in an interconnected cosmic web through which human consciousness plays a very profound role. The energy basis of illusionary matter makes the universe spring to life and negates any image of a mechanistic cosmos. Capra translates this alive world into the following appropriate imagery; "At the subatomic level the interrelations and interactions between the parts of the whole are more important than the parts themselves. There is motion but there are, ultimately, no moving objects; there is activity but there are no actors; there are no dancers, there is only the dance." (The Turning Point, Capra, P83)

7 AN ECOLOGICAL SHIFT IN PERCEPTION

If anything captures the essence of the quantum paradigm it is the inter-relatedness and inter-dependence of all phenomena in the Universe. There is, in fact, no separation and no isolation between the parts and the whole. Quantum physics has, over the last century, been established on a sound scientific footing and its technological accomplishments recognised and acknowledged in a variety of scientific fields. However, the fundamental shift in physics and its philosophical implications have yet to percolate through present day perceptions and establish as overarching an influence on our society and culture, such as the Newtonian paradigm achieved before it. In this respect, the quantum paradigm and its potential impact on our cultural and social perceptions is, in effect, a world in the making through which all who come under the influence of its fundamental tenets and principles can participate in what Jimmy Reid referred to as the 'creative re-orientation of society'. The quantum paradigm epitomizes creativity in that it upholds the principles of 'uncertainty' and 'probability'. There is nothing deterministic, certain or fixed in its conceptual vocabulary. It is governed by 'process' and is the antithesis of mechanistic. What the quantum paradigm provides is a conceptual framework through which a creative, ecological vision of humanity can evolve and challenge obsolete mechanistic perceptions of our economic and political institutions, relationships to each other and to nature itself. The vast majority of humanity, which include global elites, proceed, in the main, with a 'business as usual' mindset. They fail to see that, "Our Reality is shifting because the human world has become unstable and is no longer sustainable.... The emerging reality is radically new. We are experiencing ever more frequent and ever greater shocks and surprises, and these are not due simply to blindness and ignorance. It is our reality that is shifting. As

42

the economist Kenneth Boulding remarked, the only thing we should not be surprised at is being surprised." (Quantum Shift in the Quantum Brain, 2008, Ervin Laszlo, P 1)

Most people are now aware that climates the world over are radically changing and having serious effects on human habitation. Governments everywhere, to a lesser or greater degree, are nominally or actively engaged in taking steps to mitigate our present environmental concerns. What appears to be lacking, however, is an awareness that these concerns cannot be resolved in isolation from the systemic problems besetting a culture which predominantly focuses on, defends and subscribes to an economic and social system, derived from mechanistic principles, that enriches global and local elites at the expense of further degrading nature and exploiting its peoples. Environmental concerns are intimately connected to the capitalist system. In its relatively recent Neo-liberal incarnation, referred to by Naomi Klein as 'disaster capitalism', it is exacerbating the gulf not only between nature and mankind but the social and economic inequality between the 99%, majority and the 1%, rich and super rich. This system, in its present form, is the problem. It operates as if it had a life of its own and legitimises privatisation, deregulation and the attack on public services the world over from the crudest, survival of the fittest assumptions related more to social Darwinism than Adam Smith or Keynes. The belligerent competitiveness, opportunism and institutionalised greed of this breed of capitalist pathology fits well with extreme Darwinian theory but contradicts the essential principles and philosophy inherent in the quantum paradigm whereby all phenomena, natural and human are embedded in an interactive and interdependent complementary wholeness. It is to this interconnectedness that principles of ethical and moral values for humane, civilised social and economic living can be derived to deliver what Jimmy Reid spoke of as, a 'whole quality of life' for everyone. As a Chinese proverb warns, if we do not grasp this fading opportunity for creative, constructive change, 'we are likely to end up exactly where we are headed.'

Before looking at some of the principles and practical implications that can be derived from the quantum paradigm it is perhaps worth acknowledging the distinction between what environmentalists refer to as 'shallow' and 'deep ecology'. Shallow ecology is akin to the notion of 'objectivity' espoused by the Newtonian paradigm, in that it is anthropocentric, viewing humanity as separated from or above nature thus giving humans an ascendancy over natural kingdoms which are reduced to an 'instrumental, or use' value. Deep ecology is 'earth centred'. There is no separation between humans and the natural environment. Humanity is simply a thread in the integrated tapestry of life. Although gifted with an apparent evolving intelligence and consciousness, humanity cannot claim – despite the advances of modern science - a unique superiority over natural phenomena. Some environmentalists argue that it is this awareness of man's interdependent place in the cosmos that elicits a 'spiritual' response, not in any institutionalised religious sense, but in tune with the 'perennial philosophy' of ancient spiritual traditions whose shamans, mystics and indigenous populations celebrated an intimacy with nature that has been long lost to modern man. Scientific materialism and secular society would challenge these 'spiritual' assumptions but it is worth appreciating that the deeper quantum scientists – who included, Einstein, Heisenberg, Schroedinger, De Broglie, Jeans, Planck, Pauli and Eddington - delved into the sub- atomic world they too became 'mystics' in their own right, not in the sense that quantum physics testifies to the reality of a spiritual world, but a quantum world that left them with mystical views, spiritual questions and in awe of the cosmos. (Quantum Questions: Mystical Writings of the World's Great Physicists, Ed. By Ken Wilbur, 1984)

Deep ecology implies asking deeper questions regarding the validity of the Newtonian paradigm upon which the essence of the modern, scientific world has been built. The Newtonian world view takes for granted the scientific and economic assumptions upholding unlimited industrial growth and the materialistic society and civilisation that goes with it. When questioned from an ecological perspective, this world view is found seriously wanting. From this perspective, which is founded on the quantum reality of interconnectedness, interdependence and 'oneness', it is evident that our social, political and economic structures, institutions and technologies are based on fragmented and blinkered perceptions of reality. The social, economic and political organisations of Western civilisation are focused on outdated, exploitative, world dominating, patriarchal, racist neo-colonialism and neo-liberal capitalism, all of which are anti-ecological. Political apathy and human alienation shows that, "Old political and economic systems are crumbling or straining to breaking point. They no longer answer to our deepest needs and questions, they no longer inspire us with a vision or motivate us to action. Our relationship to nature has reached a point of global urgency. The whole mechanistic paradigm of society can no longer cope with contemporary reality." (The Quantum Society: Danah Zohar & Ian Marshall,1994, P 7)

Our perceptions are moulded from, and reinforced through, social and cultural conditioning and as Marx stated they also stem from the dominant ideas and institutions in society. Patterns of behaviour and thinking capture and determine our mindset and limit the possibilities for creating alternative social realities. Our society and culture have become so steeped in mechanistic ways of thought that superficial and trendy approaches to deep social transformation are inadequate.

Genuine social transformation demands an ecological expansion of our thinking and mindset which embraces the radical categories of process, probability, relationship and interdependence found within the conceptual framework of quantum reality. However, changing mindsets is not for the faint hearted. As Zohar and Marshall remark, "Faced with a suggestion that there is some other, some wholly different, way to perceive reality, we feel at a loss, perhaps even outraged. In the physical sciences, quantum physics has caused that kind of outrage." (Zohar and Marshall, P 17)

What appears to be required to augment and complement a quantum awareness is the kind of social outrage at the arrogance, incompetence, obscene inequality and social tragedy visited upon the world by the dominant, neo-liberal capitalist order, an order which in Latin America is now losing its once dominant influence. Only then, as reality changes on the ground, will our mindsets and perceptions truly change in unison with the new paradigm.

It is clear from the above that it is our minds, albeit conditioned and cultivated by social and cultural patterns of behaviour and thinking that determine our perceptions. So powerful have these perceptions become that the quantum revolution - all around us from laser beams, super conductors, super fluids, micro chips, a host of digital and media technologies and even the biophysics of life itself - has made little or no impact on the majority of humanity or their world view. The fact remains that unlike classical physics - which only describes a macro usefulness - quantum physics, although still an approximation in relation to what has yet to be discovered through its insights, embraces both the micro and macro worlds. Our whole way of life dictates that we live in a world of separation, isolation and distance, from each other, from the institutions and technologies that govern our lives, and from nature. Even our body language reflects this separation through our attitudes of asserting power, defensive postures or manipulative behaviour. The quantum physicist David Bohm, in his book, 'Wholeness and the Implicate Order' writes of the universe as an unbroken, harmonious wholeness. Confronting the "problem of fragmentation of human consciousness" he states, " that the widespread and pervasive distinctions between people (race, nation, family, profession, etc., etc.) which are now preventing mankind from working together for the common good, and indeed, even for survival, have one of the key factors of their origin in a kind of thought that treats things as inherently divided, disconnected, and 'broken up' into yet smaller constituent parts. Each part is considered to be essentially independent and self existent.... If he thinks of

the totality as constituted of independent fragments, then that is how his mind will tend to operate." He concludes this assessment by arguing that seeing the world as a coherent, harmonious, undivided, unbroken, wholeness will create, eventually, a perceptive consciousness or awareness from which "an orderly action within the whole" of an integrated reality will flow.
(Wholeness and the Implicate Order, David Bohm, 1980, P X1)

8 COMMUNITY: THE SOURCE OF HUMANE VALUES

Unfortunately, it is not only a radical shift in our perceptions and thinking that is required but a fundamental change in our morals, values and ethics. The predominant values of Western society are those that cultivate self-assertion over social cohesion and integration, competition over cooperation and domination over partnership. All living systems display these opposite tendencies which are in themselves neither good or bad. The natural world encourages a healthy, dynamic balance between these elements. Western industrial culture emphasises an unhealthy, self-assertiveness which creates an imbalance at the expense of integrated, cohesive ways of social living and personal, responsible behaviour. The following table illustrates these opposing tendencies in ways of thinking and values that conflict if one tendency comes to dominate our thinking, behaviour and actions.

THINKING		VALUES	
Self-Assertive	Integrative	Self-Assertive	Integrative
rational	intuitive	expansion	conservation
analysis	synthesis	competition	cooperation
reductionist	holistic	quantity	quality
linear	non-linear	domination	partnership

(The Web of Life: A New Synthesis of Mind and Matter: Fritjof Capra, 1996, P. 10)

It is clear from the above that a culture based on a holistic balance between the self-assertive and the integrative elements would be more socially productive, just and compassionate and lead to more contentment and happiness. The concept of 'network' as opposed to hierarchical structures is an appropriate metaphor in tune with the new quantum paradigm. Indeed, 'network' is the principle metaphor representative of ecological harmony and from such harmony a new set of humane, dignified values and ethical systems would emerge.

For the most part humanity lives in hierarchical societies, generally patriarchal in nature. The values of competition, expansion and domination are characteristically male associated, inducing a mindset difficult to shift. Identities of place and station are moulded from the acceptance of hierarchies as the natural order of social arrangements. The neo-liberal economy has reinforced hierarchy not in any traditional class sense but in establishing the elitist 'corporate state' as the overarching economic structure through which all our institutions are subsumed under and to which we have been conditioned to pay homage to. This is reflected in the recent compliance of Governments and elected politicians taking critical decisions, ostensibly to safeguard the electorate, but more to save corporate banks and financial institutions from their own greed and incompetence during the 'credit crunch'. Neo-liberal corporate ideology could not have taken root in our minds were it not for Milton Friedman's political accomplices across the world, some of whom were brutal dictators. The demise of the Soviet Union provided the impetus not only for the 'liberation' of free-markets from cold war constraints but was the catalyst to deliberately socially engineer societies to conform with Friedman's doctrine of laissez faire, unfettered capitalism. In Britain, this process reinforced and multiplied all the personal traits and social characteristics criticised and indicted by Jimmy Reid in his1972 Rectorial address.

Neo-liberal ideology was dependent on specific geographical circumstances. It came to be applied differently in different countries, especially in response to natural disasters, political opportunities and emerging dictatorships, as was the case in Latin America. Its ideologues worked from the assumption that the unfettered, free-market creed would in time create an imprinted mindset compatible with its basic principles. This individualistic mindset was taken to new levels by the Chicago School doctrine and fitted well with right-wing governments, which in the British instance, left the country, more self-assertive and less cohesive, more rootless and morally bankrupt at every level, especially at the upper echelons of society where institutional corruption became more prevalent. The social consequences of what David Cameron referred to as a 'moral collapse', exacerbated the gradual demise of our sense of community and shared identity. Our frenetic, fragmented, self-assertive lifestyles together with the social pathology of opulent affluence, obscene inequality and deprivation, smothered youthful idealism and drove whole communities of young people into the nihilistic despair of drugs, alcohol and gang culture, with all the domestic, social and urban violence that went with it.

'Thatcherism', epitomized Friedman's and Hayek's dogma in Britain. It played the dominant role in conditioning and cultivating excessive, individualistic attitudes which has apparently sucked all existential meaning from our lives, with the exception of money, conspicuous consumption, heaving debts and increasing narcissism. Those born during this time became known as 'Thatcher's Children', such was the potency of the self-assertive changes that took place in her name and through which a generation of young people were infected with her winner takes all, 'greed is good', creed. What such 'social engineering' shows is the immense power of conditioning that springs from ideas that become dominant in society when pushed with theological fervour and decisive political action. What it also demonstrates is the real possibility of changing perceptions, mindsets and values when people are positively persuaded of the validity of a more socially cohesive way of living that is supported by scientific principles rather than economic dogma.

Human values and humane ethical systems are the essence of an ecological approach to ushering in the new quantum paradigm. What the general collapse in our values demonstrates is that its focus is 'human centred' while deep ecology is 'earth centred' which gives an ingrained value to both human and non-human existence. All sentient life forms live in a 'network' of interdependent ecological communities. When human beings become aware that nature is the ground of their whole being and survival on this planet and not simply a separate dominion for material exploitation then perceptions will change and an ethical renaissance will come into being and transform our way of living and our relationship with the earth and each other. No where is this new 'eco-ethical' awareness so necessary than in modern science where the decisions taken are often life threatening rather than life enhancing. The development of weapons systems, chemical contamination, questionable pharmaceutical drugs and biological crop and animal experimentation are but some of the negative aspects of science when locked into a hierarchical system which sets priorities in tune with the dominant economic and political mindset. These developments are in contrast to the many biology TV programmes that demonstrate an ecological awareness of life as an integrated, interdependent whole but which tend to see the human species as a special living form observing an objective world. The notion of 'objective observer' is integral to the Newtonian paradigm and as such regards values as separate from scientific facts, a principle completely undermined by quantum revelations which shows that there is no such thing as objective, value- free science. Scientific facts which combine perceptions, values and actions cannot be viewed out with the paradigm in which they are integrally immersed. Scientists are, therefore, intellectually and morally responsible for the outcomes of their research.

In the ecological world view, nature itself, being the ground of our sustainable existence, becomes the source of all our values. The quantum paradigm has confirmed the 'oneness' of the web of life. From this perspective the human 'self' becomes identified with the natural order in a way that helps to expand awareness of the interdependencies between nature and all life forms.

This should, with time, preclude him or her from, theoretically at least, damaging the ground they are literally standing on. As Arne Naes remarks; "Care flows naturally if the 'self' is widened and deepened so that protection of free Nature is felt and conceived as protection of ourselves....Just as we need no morals to make us breathe...(so) if your 'self' in the wide sense embraces another being, you need no moral exhortation to show care....If reality is like it is experienced by the ecological self, our behaviour naturally and beautifully follows norms of strict environmental ethics" (Quoted in The Web of Life; Fritjof Capra: 1996 P. 12) It is ,of course, one thing to be logically and intellectually aware that we are an integral part of the natural environment. It is another thing to have a psychologically deep, ecological awareness which will makes us more inclined to care and honour the living natural order as if it were our own extended self and body. The idea of the eco-self has been supported in the writings of Joanna Macy who talks of the 'greening of the self' while Warwick Fox has developed the theme as 'transpersonal ecology'. Ecological reality is a vision of life which embraces James Lovelock's Gaia hypothesis that the earth itself is not only metaphorically, a living, breathing entity, but a harmonious biological reality. The earth is so finely balanced that today's relentless industrial technologies are now taking a devastating toll in terms of both resources and human life, including the dysfunctions visited upon the wider social environment.

A social and economic vision based on ecological values and ethics would bring forth a world rooted in the concept of community. Ideally, a community would stretch from a local grass roots base - which gives the idea its authenticity as a democratic spring board - to national, international and global community networks. Together, these networks would reinforce the values of an ethics based eco-system confirming that the whole is greater than the sum of the parts. One of the major problems to be overcome in our highly, self-assertive society is how to balance person-hood and individuality with public communal involvement that diminishes neither. How, in effect, do we safeguard diversity, in all its manifestations, within a transcendent vision of a global eco-community? Danah Zohar addresses this question this way, "Each of us experiences ourselves as an individual with personal truth,....Yet at the same time we feel that we only truly know ourselves, only truly become ourselves, through the complex set of relations that bind us to nature, to others with whom we are in daily commerce, and to the culture of which we are part. Our individuality, we feel can never be wholly exhausted, but neither, we recognise, can it ever be wholly isolated." (The Quantum Society: Danah Zohar & Ian Marshall: 1993, P. 64)

It is relationship, that binds our individuality to each other, to our culture, and to nature, giving in the process a sense of psychological comfort, completeness and wholeness. Self-serving values are rupturing our social and cultural fabric and displacing our sense of community, cooperation and service with an outdated Darwinian, 'survival of the fittest' competitiveness. These over assertive values contradict the overarching, harmony and balance which exists in the natural order and in human communities, given the appropriate social, cultural and environmental nourishment. Scratch a human community, even when fragmented and riven apart by a destructive economic system and it will reveal a caring, sharing heart. This is clear from communities across the world, especially those where injustice strikes the hardest in places like the Favela's in Latin America and the Townships of South Africa.

Communities, given the freedom and opportunity, are representative of the natural order of life itself. Harmonious, self- organising communities exist within nature, ranging from big cats, to fish, to birds, and to insects. A global ecological community could ideally emerge, based on natural principles, inherent values and structures that in the absence of a dysfunctional economic system has the possibility of creating the most advantageous way to survive in a world forever in the state of flux, change and impermanence. Human communities have been in existence from time immemorial. As humanity evolved, isolated communities gravitated together forming agrarian and urban communities and with an expansion of trade and commerce formed networks of interconnecting communities, all pulling in the direction of the present 'world wide web' global community. History and anthropology reflects the expansion of the human community as an integral part of a wider order of life's natural integrative processes. Critics will argue that nature is 'raw in tooth and claw' when referring to the 'law of the jungle' scenes portrayed by big cats hunting and tearing their prey. This is not premeditated exploitation of their prey but nature's way of maintaining a balanced equilibrium or wholeness, done without motivation of revenge or other falsely created rationalisation for conflict as perpetrated by reasoning human beings.

The ecological community not only provides the conceptual framework on which to base human values and ethics but confirms the essence of the quantum paradigm. This is a reality governed by a network of complex relationships and interdependencies that transcend artificial, mechanistic boundaries. Viewing the world from the perspective of natural organisms, including humans, it becomes very clear that each organism is an integrated whole in its own right and thus a living system. Although living organisms do have machine-like parts and exhibit machine like behaviour this cannot account for their organismic or systemic nature. Wholeness also applies to animal and insect social systems like buffalo herds, anthills, beehives and even human families. Whether it is a bacterium, plant, animal or human they are all an expression of a living system whose survival is dependent on the complexity of their mutual interactions and relationships. Systems biology, which implies interactive, interdependent relationships within the context of community, offers a systems approach to understanding living communities. This approach is more in tune with a reality based on process as opposed to that of mechanism. However, even within this framework there is still a place for a reductionist methodology to enhance our understanding of the living world, "The reductionist description of organisms can therefore be useful and may in some cases be necessary. It is dangerous only when it is taken to be the complete explanation. Reductionism and holism, analysis and synthesis, are complementary approaches that, used in proper balance, help us obtain a deeper knowledge of life." (F. Capra: The Turning Point: 1982, P. 288)

9 MATERIALISM AND SOCIAL ENGINEERING

Deep ecological values are based on the ideal of 'community' whether local, national or global. The concept also embodies the idea of integrating human communities with planet Earth, the only genuine resource for guaranteeing our survival. Community based values provide the human framework to promote a paradigm shift through which the political, economic and social needs of humanity can be addressed in harmony with the natural order. This framework encourages a holistic balance between self-assertive and integrative thinking and values. This contrasts with and contradicts the predominant self-assertive thinking and values that are the foundation of our present materialist based culture. Intimately linked to the corrosive, individualistic values inherent in materialist culture is the economic drive for unlimited economic growth. Indeed, the pursuit of unlimited growth is deliberately fed by the artificial creation of demand through incessant advertising and the impulse for product innovation. In the event, materialism has reduced humanity to B.F. Skinner's crude 'stimulus and response' behaviourism, which, in its philosophy, was to socially engineer humanity's 'false' and 'aberrant' habits out of existence and introduce another 'brave new world'.

The psychological theories lurking behind materialism are subtle forms of behaviourism which have been associated with ideas of authoritarianism, conformity and social control. Behaviourist techniques have socio-political and ideological implications which cannot be separated from the behaviourist concept of man, shaped, manipulated and programmed, ostensibly for his own betterment. Skinner's contention was that if man was subject to such shaping then he ought to be shaped in ways which will improve his well being and culture. Thus, " The primary role of society....is to set up planned, systematic reinforcement contingencies....Since humans are malleable behavioural engineering is the crux of the matter." (Three Views of Man: R.D. Nye, 1975, P138/139.) Skinner's novel Walden 11, is an account of how society, using positive and negative contingencies of reinforcement, could be socially engineered to include 'peaceful', 'co-operative' and 'considerate' behaviours.

Behavioural engineering, however, has the potential for promoting conformity and adjustment to what society considers to be 'normal'. The employment of any sophisticated, behavioural psychological techniques has the potential to implant state of the art ideas and images. In this way, "The individual loses his active, responsible role in the social process; he becomes completely 'adjusted' and learns that any behavioural act, thought or feeling which does not fit into the general scheme puts him at a severe disadvantage." (From E.,The Anatomy of Human Destructiveness, 1973, P. 73) Like so many thinkers with admirable intentions, Skinner's ideas were not only flawed but socially dangerous. He wanted " a world where people feel free as they have never felt before....in which people achieve more than ever before. I want people to feel tremendously worthy." (Skinner B. F. quoted in Cohen D. Psychologists on Psychology, 1977, P. 267). Irrespective of what Skinner wanted or indeed what modern behavioural advertising techniques are designed to achieve, the end result is that those in corporate power dictate the behaviours and reinforcements they wish to implant in order to shape and manipulate society in any ideological direction. Over the last thirty years neo-liberal capitalism has used social engineering to implant its ideologically motivated political and economic strategies. It is no accident that forms of behaviourism emerged in America. It is the self-appointed keeper of the capitalist, liberal tradition and the ideological optimism inherent in it. Neo-liberalism has literally taken the capitalist baton to its ideological conclusion and structured and designed a society primarily for corporations, financiers, bankers, the super rich, compliant politicians and celebrities, with the people playing supporting, productive and consumer roles.

As it has turned out, neo-liberal capitalism is a world of addicted consumers controlled by trans-national corporations. Corporations themselves are afflicted by an addiction that Walter Hume in the Scottish Review referred to as O C G, 'obsessive compulsive greed'. All addictions are obsessive and compulsive. In psychiatrists language, consumerism is a 'psychopathology', an addiction that can be traced back to childhood. According to Mike Searles, President of 'Kids 'R' Us', " if you own this child at an early age, you can own this child for years to come. Companies are saying, 'Hey, I want to own the kid younger and younger and younger'." (Quoted in, The High Price Of Materialism, Tim Kasser, 2002, P. 91) These corporations have no qualms about growing, owning or targeting the most emotionally vulnerable in society. A 2007 UNICEF study, led by Agnes Nairn of the EM-Lyon Business School in France, revealed that in relation to child well-being, Britain distinguished itself by coming bottom of the league among twenty one industrialised countries. In a comparison with Sweden and Spain it was found that British parents were under greater pressure to purchase for themselves and their children. The report stated that, "Boxes of toys, broken presents and unused electronics in the home were witness to this drive to acquire new possessions." (UNICEF study quoted in the Sunday Herald, 'How We Sold Our Souls', Judith Duffy, 15.04.12)

Dr. Carol Craig, CEO of the 'Centre for Confidence and Well-Being' believes that materialism and celebrity are having such a dominating and distorting effect on our lives and values that she has now written a book on it. (Carol Craig,The Great Takeover, How materialism, the media and markets now dominate our lives,2012) According to Dr. Craig, we no longer compare ourselves with our neighbours but with, "global celebrity culture....and those deemed to be the most beautiful, talented or rich." (Quoted in Sunday Herald, 15.04.12) The UNICEF report emphasised that the socially devastating aspect of the 'hauling' phenomenon was the economic impact on poorer families who are the group most likely to suffer. " Some of the work....

shows quite clearly it is the children who can't afford designer brands are the ones that really want them and the same goes for the parents....That has a terrible impact as you end up with families who spend all their money on IPads and so forth and can't afford the rent." (UNICEF study,quoted in Sunday Herald, 15.04.12) In this context, the latest possessions appear to bolster confidence and identity. Roger Scruton, the philosopher tends to see constant consumption as an integral root of our 'social ills' while another philosopher Julian Baggini remarks that we see other peoples materialism but not our own. Carol Craig likened the problem to that confronting the 18th Century Scottish Enlightenment scholars who wanted to demolish the malaise of their time, the irrational beliefs in 'superstition' and 'religious fanaticism'. "We need a similar project of enlightenment, we need to shine the light into dark places. These dark places are these toxic base values....that are undermining our environment,.... and diminishing our lives." (Dr. Carol Craig, quoted in Sunday Herald, 15.04.12)

Abraham Maslow's gradations of psychological hierarchies places security and physical needs on the bottom rung. He believed that human beings were hard wired for growth and development and in time, through experience and learning, would consciously evolve by stages to the highest realm, the 'peak' of which was 'self-actualisation'. Carl Rogers, another humanist psychologist, held the same view as Jimmy Reid which was a staunch, "....faith in humanity. All that is good in man's heritage involves recognition of our common humanity, an unashamed acknowledgement that man is good by nature." (Glasgow Rectorial Address 1972, Jimmy Reid) What stands in the way of self fulfilment and closer personal relationships with others are the 'toxic base values' that Carol Craig writes about; those very same values promulgated by the manipulative ideologies of neo-liberal capitalism, Thatcherite conservatism and radical behaviourism. These retrograde ideologies stand together and blunt our perceptions and awareness of the potential for social change. Under these systems the majority of human beings are reduced to automatons and stuck at the lowest rung of Maslow's psychological ladder in fear, insecurity and the metaphorical, materialist 'rat-race'.

Contemporary studies have shown that the psychological need for acquiring material goods is rooted in fear, insecurity and personal safety. For the majority of people, security and personal safety are never fully met under an unstable economic system that periodically breaks down. These needs are also never adequately met for those who are the beneficiaries of the system, especially in today's conditions where lucrative employment can end immediately. "From this perspective, materialist values are both a symptom of underlying insecurity and a coping strategy (albeit a relatively ineffective one) some people use in an attempt to alleviate their anxieties." (The High Price of Materialism: Tim Kasser, 2002, P.29) Family circumstances, local communities, national culture and global trends all have a socialising influence which stamp their values and habits on the individual. In the last three decades we have been exposed to particularly virulent, self-serving attitudes and a mindset that runs contrary to man's higher natural inclinations for self-esteem, belongingness, community and compassion for others.

According to Danah Zohar, materialism is a 'pathological expression' or 'a distorted quest for meaning'. " We can see this at the personal, and even at the political, level, in the rush into materialism, in the vain quest for meaning in the acquisition of 'things' or wealth as empty symbols of self or identity or power" (The Quantum Society: Danah Zohar & Ian Marshall, P.217/230) There may be a contradiction at the heart of the neo-liberal and conservative alliance. The former, extols the virtues of self-assertiveness which has shredded the social fabric, while the latter ostensibly wishes to hold on to the ideas of traditional community, family and religious values; a prime example of this in Britain being David Cameron's 'Big Society'. In practice, both ideologies have sacrificed the public domain and democracy itself and created societies whereby people turn to products rather than political processes to find solutions for their fears and insecurities.

The addiction to materialism has not only an affect on personal health and well-being but on relationships with partners, children, neighbours, society and ultimately the earth itself. Driven by the desire for wealth, power, status, celebrity and personal image, our behaviour takes on an aggressive, competitive edge, the very values that give our present capitalist economy its raison d'etre. In the process, and even against our better nature and rational mind, we develop tendencies which tears the social and community fabric apart thus isolating, alienating and breeding conformity. These tendencies are the very antithesis of what is deemed possible within the conceptual framework of the Quantum paradigm where there is found connectedness, inter-relationship and interaction and no isolation and separation. In a society geared to unlimited growth, those who hold ultimate power, wealth and status become the goal setters for the whole society.

The elite's materialistic affluence and influence percolates down to the social bedrock and encourages behaviour which the 'establishment' brands anti-social. This behaviour simply reflects the desperate response of deprived sections of the community. The recent urban riots in England testified to this dysfunctional, but induced behaviour. Cash nexus, corporate values can be seen in excessive bonus payouts, chief executives salaries, management attitudes towards employees and the increasing gulf in inequality. When 'merit pay' was cut for Chrysler employees the chief executive granted himself a $20 million bonus and later commented, "That's the American way. If little kids don't aspire to make money like I did, what the hell good is this country." (quoted in, The High Price of Materialism, Tim Kasser, P.90) Attitudes like this, stemming from materialistic values have lost any intrinsic meaning other than the abuse of power and corporate greed, institutionalised by widespread corruption and an economic and political establishment that can no longer hold claim to its democratic credentials.

If materialism has a deleterious affect on human health, behavioural patterns, social unrest and cultural values, it has had a greater impact on the earth's ecosystem. Excessive consumption in the West exacerbates the economic and political divisions between the underdeveloped and developed worlds and the growing economic gulf between the super rich and the rest of us. It also highlights the pace at which water, forests, clean air and the Earth's resources in general are being polluted and utilised to satisfy an insatiable, artificially created demand. It is not only large populations in great swathes of the world that are being exploited, punished and denied the benefits of these resources to satisfy a very modest lifestyle, it is the damage to the diversity of whole ecosystems. "In regard to both the physical and the biological resources of the planet, the rising curve of demand is exceeding the descending curve of supply....in the six decades since World War 11, humanity has consumed more of the planet's physical and biological resources than in all of history prior to that time. Global consumption is nearing planetary limits." (Quantum Shift in the Global Brain, Ervin Laszlo, P. 42)

The alienation from major economic and political institutions, now experienced in Western society runs parallel with our alienation from nature itself. This is evident from Australian and other surveys which showed that those who pursued materialistic values the most, "reported negative attitudes towards the environment, little love of all living things, and few ecologically friendly behaviours." (Shaun Saunders and Dan Munro, Quoted in The High Price of Materialism, Tim Kasser, P.92) Given the present materialistic orientation of Western society and the rising economies of India, China and Brazil reaching out to emulate Western 'standards of living', it is clear that a finite planet cannot sustain such profligacy. The economic drive to unlimited growth not only contradicts the earth's finite material resources but the very principles of the Quantum paradigm. Scientifically, the paradigm sustains the premise that ecological harmony, unity and oneness are the established constants of quantum reality and if or when this harmony is seriously disrupted, nature, given time, which the universe has plenty of, will bring the planet back to stasis at any human cost. The Earth or Gaia is now in the process of communicating this fact through fire, flood, famine and species extinction along with any other means of showing that planetary and human harmony is not now an option but an imperative. This is now the stance of Serge Latouche's, book, 'Farewell to Growth'. As an arch-critic of unlimited growth – a subject which is both complicated and controversial - Latouche focuses on the political, economic and social dimensions of the subject and for this reason his critique will be used in the next section as a way of highlighting the problems involved and looking at the viability of strategies for future survival.

It is ironic that Skinner, in excluding mental processes from his behavioural psychology, invested a disproportionate amount of time experimenting with rats to demonstrate the validity of his theory. This was the very same mammal Jimmy Reid vociferously argued in his Rectorial Address that human beings were most definitely not. In practice, the modern corporation has adopted more subtle stimulus and response techniques than Skinner's by getting inside the consumer's head or mental processes and psychologically projecting the images of affluence, status, sex, desire, feelings and emotions, those very characteristics that are declared to give us the perception that we are part of what life's goal is all about. Due to its effectiveness, these forms of behaviourism are even more manipulative, deterministic and mechanistic than even Skinner could ever have imagined.

10 EARTH CENTRED JUSTICE

Western civilisation is still rooted in the 19th Century idea of progress. This was a time when capital accumulation, technological innovation, colonial acquisition and imperial domination gave the promise of a bright future for European and American expansion. To achieve this, whole continents, cultures and indigenous societies were hijacked and plundered for the economic and political benefit of the West. This is the foundation of the West's continuing economic dominance over the third world and industrial capitalism's continuing quest for material resources to feed an insatiable need for unlimited growth and economic expansion. The development of Western civilisation over the last four hundred years can be summed up as the four C's, conquest, colonisation, competition and consumption. Such 'progress' is driven by an aggressive economic system, the raison d'etre of which is an economic obsession with undifferentiated growth, delivering over time zero sustainability. This inherent compulsion to expand is the 'darker' side of capitalism, which, in its present corporate form, has come to dominate the planet at the expense of ecological viability, the corruption of our political institutions, national sovereignty, personal health and democracy itself. Although still controversial in economic discourse, it is becoming clear to those more influenced by ecological science that quantitative growth is no longer sustainable on a finite planet whatever technologies are developed to mitigate the excesses of corporate capitalism. According to Ervin Laszlo, growth on this level and at this rate is not a benign planetary health risk, "Unrestrained, purely quantitative growth in energy and materials production and consumption is not possible on a finite planet with finite resources and a delicately balanced biosphere: ultimately it is bound to deflect and then turn into growth of a cancerous kind." (Quantum Shift in the Global Brain, Ervin Laszlo, P. 47)

Despite our awareness over a long period of time that the theoretical economic roots of unlimited growth are questionable, most of us, including economists, have shunted its implications into the hinterlands of our minds. Stretching as far back as Rachel Carson's 'Silent Spring', through the warnings from The Club of Rome's report on 'The Limits to Growth' and its updates, followed by the 'Intergovernmental Experts' Report' from Greenpeace, Friends of the Earth and other environmental bodies, to the damning film from Al Gore, their collective revelations have made only an intellectual and visual impact on our lives. According to Serge Latouche, we live in "a society that has been swallowed up by an economy whose only goal is growth for the sake of growth." (Farewell to Growth, Serge Latouche, 2009, P. 3) There is, in fact, very little criticism in 'environmentalist discourses' or conventional economic thinking regarding the dominant status of economic growth in comparison with vague references to sustainable development. " Denunciations of the 'frenzy of human activity' or of the enthusiasm for the word 'progress' are no substitute for an analysis of the capitalist and techno-economic marketing mega-machine. We are cogs in that machine, and we may well collude with it, but we are definitely not the driving force behind it. This system is based upon excess, and it is leading us into a blind alley." (Serge Latouche, 2009, P.3).

The grand irony is that addictive consumerism is so pervasive in Western societies that it is difficult to visualise, far less accept the necessity for dramatic reductions in production and consumption. In fact, " Nothing contradicts capitalism's constitutive imperative towards growth more than the concept of rationing goods and resources. Yet it is becoming uncomfortably clear that consumer self-regulation and the market will not by themselves avert environmental catastrophe." (Capitalist Realism: Is There No Alternative?, Mark Fisher, 2009, P. 80) We are, indisputably, trapped in a corporate, economic and financial system through which the indicators of growth, consumption and employment become the principle measurements of progress and prosperity. These three dominant economic characteristics complete a circle from which all else, including assumptions behind social justice and happiness, are quantified. The circle, unfortunately, is a vicious one which is broken periodically by the inherent instability of the free market system, followed by the inevitable social consequences. The present economic crash, triggered by the 2008 'credit crunch', was, however, the ultimate circuit breaker which created the 'perfect economic storm' and alerted the world's populations to the devastating, systemic dysfunction of unfettered corporate capitalism, in its most aggressive, neo-liberal form, which has raised an awareness regarding the questionable economic and ethical justification for its continued existence. Indeed, in America, classical capitalism and its constitutionally declared pursuit of happiness has evolved into a degenerate, neo-liberal corporatism and its unashamed pursuit of extortionate wealth and 'managed democracy'.

Britain has now lost the hallowed triple rating and descended into an economic pit. Economists from centre left and centre right are still advocating either government stimulated or austerity growth approaches as a way out of this malaise. Both approaches, due to orthodox economic thinking, combined with electoral pressures on governments to gain or retain political office, suffer from the locked in growth syndrome. At this moment in time, with the increasing gulf in inequality and the crisis in unemployment, there appears to be little option but for governments, trade unions and political parties to repair the economic circle and once again launch the economy in the direction of growth, jobs and consumption and another cycle of 'boom and bust'. However, is this not the moment, when the neo-liberal state has been apparently, struck down and weakened by its own contradictions, arrogant incompetence and inherent greed, to challenge its flawed ideological roots and established structures? Fisher believes that this is an opportune time to make such a challenge even in the knowledge that the credit crunch will not be the end of capitalism, "....the crisis has led to the relaxing of a certain kind of mental paralysis. We are now in a political landscape littered with what Alex Williams called 'ideological rubble' – it is year zero again, and a space has been cleared for a new anti-capitalism to emerge which is not necessarily tied to the old language or traditions....Anti-capitalism must oppose Capital's globalism with its own, authentic, universality." (M. Fisher, P. 78/80) The question brought to mind in launching this challenge is how far have the trade unions and labour movements themselves been seriously undermined and institutionally weakened over the last thirty years from the onslaught of neo-liberal governments and anti-labour legislation? With or without traditional trade union and labour movement support, social unrest and protest is everywhere spreading in increasing numbers and involving a spontaneous cohesive blending of a variety of social groupings from disappointed middle class participants to students, workers and slum dwellers. Here Paul Mason captures the essence and the breadth of this revolt, " The boom years of globalization created a mass, transnational culture of being young and educated; now there is a mass transnational culture of disillusionment. And it transmits easily.....From the rich world to the poor world, it is educated young people whose life chances and illusions are now being shattered. Though their general conditions are still better than those of slum-dwellers and some workers, they have experienced far greater disappointed " (Paul Mason, Why it's Kicking Of Everywhere: The New Global Revolutions, 2012, P's 69&72)

Austerity programmes and the more conventional Keynesian growth solutions are rooted in a reductive, mechanistic, conceptual framework. These economic systems are generally dominated by unrealistic, formulaic, economic models. Generally, they are based on the classical ideal of free markets functioning in harmony with supply and demand but operated external and blind to ecological considerations, including the full local,social and health costs of production. Since transnational corporations have extended their dominance over the supply of goods, artificially created demand and decisive political influence over government policies, they have long nullified the validity of any concept of classical free market theory or practice, including that of the more beneficial Keynesian, mixed economy solution. If we take into consideration the current ecological plight of the planet and the majority of its inhabitants, the present dire circumstances is the appropriate time to re-examine questions related to delivering a 'whole quality of life', which includes social justice, ethical values, and a vision as to where, in the long term, western civilisation and global culture is heading. Poverty and deprivation in the underdeveloped world and its relative but growing counterpart in Western societies demands that a modern economy be sound ecologically, economically viable and socially and ethically responsible. Sustainable growth, compatible with planetary and human needs, as opposed to artificially created, superfluous materialist wants, has now, it would appear, become essential for human survival.

The idea of the limits to growth can be traced back to Malthus and before that to Adam Smith and John Stuart Mill. It was, however, through the work of the Romanian scientist and economist, Georgescu-Roegen that realised the economic connection with ecology, particularly in the context of the law of entropy and its bio-economic implications. In brief, working within classical Newtonian mechanics, economists have ignored the law of entropy - that is the non-reversibility of energy and matter - thus divorcing the earth's ecology from human productive activity and opening the ecological gates to unlimited economic production. Being indifferent or ignorant of the laws of physics, biology, chemistry and, especially, the laws of thermodynamics, masks the interdependence between economics and the biosphere. In the words of Serge Latouche, "It is ecological nonsense. The real economic process, unlike the theoretical model, is not, in short, a purely mechanical and reversible process; it is by its very nature entropic and takes place in a biosphere that functions within a temporality that is not reversible." (Serge Latouche, P. 15) The economist, Kenneth Boulding recognised the implications of the problem as far back as 1966 when he contrasted our predatory 'cowboy economy', which plundered and pillaged natural resources, with the finite 'spaceman economy'.And for those who could not see the lunacy of indefinite growth, Boulding concluded that they were either madmen or economists.

An example of this madness can be seen in one economist's outlook for the future. As long as the sun shines, "there are no unavoidable 'scientific' limits to the development of economic activity on earth...." Ecological disasters set off by any human activity can be corrected by making, "even more progress towards understanding and mastering our environment. And to make the world even more artificial." (Guillaume Duval, quoted in Farewell to Growth, Serge Latouche P.21) The phrase, 'mastering our environment' is the clue confirming values, attitudes and a mindset derived from an outdated 19th century ideal of limitless progress. Mastering nature goes back to Bacon and Descartes and is the product of the theoretical adaptation of economics to the Newtonian paradigm, which, unlike the quantum paradigm, excludes the earth's ecological interdependencies with human social activity from its scientific calculations and practical considerations. As stressed by Latouche, "The ancient wisdom of living in harmony with an environment that we exploit in reasonable ways has given way to hubris, or the overweening pride of the masters and possessors of nature. This quantitative madness will inevitably make our lives unbearable..." (Latouche, P. 21)

Latouche, is one of the most forthright critics of unlimited economic growth. His concept of 'de-growth' has been referred to as an 'explosive word' or as he says, a 'political slogan' through which to mount a challenge to the economic orthodoxy of exponential growth. This is a goal which reduces human beings to an "instrument... used by the productive mechanism" and so become 'waste products' of the system. (Latouche, P. 8) His blunt critique of unlimited growth emphasises that 'de-growth' is not negative growth but a rallying call for those who offer a fundamental alternative to the "quasi-idolatrous cult of growth for growth's sake". De-growth, "is an essential proposition if we are to open up a space for the inventiveness and creativity of the imagination, which has been blocked by economistic, developmentalist and progressive totalitarianism." (Latouche, P. 9) The language may appear extreme, but when a recent book by a respected American political philosopher also uses the word 'totalitarianism' in its title with respect to democracy, it crystallizes the depth and breadth of the ecological, cultural and democratic dilemma confronting Western civilisation in particular and humanity as a whole. (Democracy Incorporated: Managed Democracy, and the Specter of Inverted Totalitarianism, Sheldon Wolin)

Latouche also criticises the concept of sustainability as no more than 'verbal diplomacy'. He links the idea to technologies that save energy and reduce carbon emissions while sustaining Western promoted, exploitative growth and development strategies. Latouche, unabashedly, declares that the concept of 'de-growth' is about creating a 'utopia' in our consciousness to further the 'possibility of its implementation'. "De-growth is therefore a political project in the strong sense of the term. It means building convivial societies that are autonomous and economical in both the North and South.... It cannot be contained within the arena of mere politicking, and is designed to restore politics to its full dignity. It is a quest for an overall theoretical coherence" (Latouche, P.32) To achieve a theoretical coherence, which appears to be totally absent from growth economics, Latouche proposes a synthesis of eight interdependent strategies for change which he calls the 'virtuous circles' of eight 'R's'. They are, re-evaluate, re-conceptualise, restructure, redistribute, re-localise, reduce, re-use and re-cycle. Under the heading of 're-evaluate, Latouche calls for a complete re-orientation of our values. He views the value of 'altruism' over egotism and competition as the way to encourage cooperation from which more humane values could be derived. But the key value upon which all his 'virtuous circles' focus, is to live in harmony with nature and replace our dominant, predatory mindset.

While Latouche's eight R's are theoretically coherent in a strategic, political sense, they also require a sound re-evaluation of the science behind an ecological approach to the question of growth. There can be no clear answers or empirical proof of the sustainability of a global economy projected into the future, but observations, theoretical analysis and the entropy laws of thermodynamics suggest that we are fast approaching the limits of the planet's ability to respond to human need, or as is the case today, human greed. If this is the case, then as Einstein once remarked, problems cannot be resolved using the same economic or scientific thinking that created the problem in the first place. Orthodox capitalist economics, in its various guises, is an 'extractive science' which basically transforms natural resources into commodities and services for consumption without ensuring the regeneration of the natural world for present or future generations. This economics is one dimensional in that it can see no further than satisfying artificially created consumer demands, profit levels and scarcity management. The only value it perceives is the exchange cash value of a commodity, whether it be a product or a wage exploited human. Present day capitalist economics is above all a reductionist science which fails to deal with the holistic wholeness of the ecological world within which it operates.

Whatever Latouche's reservations are over the concept of sustainability, our prime focus at present ought to be on curbing the excesses of human productive and consumptive activity. This would help to sustain the planet's ability to thrive and regenerate. The quantum paradigm is multi-dimensional and embraces all that is, where humanity is but 'a strand in the web of life', which, according to quantum physics extends in an unbroken continuity beyond the planet to the universe and the cosmos. The economics of Newtonian mechanistic principles are no longer valid in the paradoxical world of quantum probabilities, uncertainty principles and the complementarity of wave/particle duality; a world whose scientific foundations have undergone a revolutionary shift and whose evolutionary principles are based on wholeness, interconnectedness, dynamic interdependencies and process. Quantum science would provide Latouche with the 'theoretical coherence' he requires, not only to reinforce his eight R's but any other economic and political strategies that will evolve in the future to support a deep ecological approach to human and planetary survival.

Latouche, in the end, admits that his proposals are an 'intellectual construct', a utopian presentation of an ideal way forward. By themselves they would not crack capitalist economic orthodoxy on the question of growth. Although he states that his proposals are not a 'political project' he does emphasise that his concept of 'de-growth' captures the imagination of the ecologists 'old slogan of think globally, act locally'. In other words, Latouche's utopia can only be realised through the local involvement of people at the grass roots level around the world and he goes into some detail on issues like, 'Inventing Local Ecological Democracy'. Naomi Klein and Raj Patel provide clear evidence that local, community based movements to find better ways of organised living are evolving in Latin America and else where. The emphasis on local action highlights the need for local democracy, innovation and networked organisation, not hierarchies which is what capitalist elites benefit from and practice at present. Although Latouche presents an ideal utopian transformation he is very aware that what he is saying embodies a potential 'revolutionary' edge. He is convinced that in any transformation of this nature there is a need for pragmatic political action so long as the end result does not, "degenerate into compromises at the intellectual level." (Latouche, P. 66) Against his better judgement, Latouche has to admit that if his ideal is to manifest a new ecological reality it has to become a political programme which involves 'electoral issues' carried out by politicians who do not have a holistic understanding of the problem and cannot be trusted as they are mere 'functionaries' of a "dictatorship of the financial markets". (Duclos, 1997, quoted in Latouche, p. 68) To achieve a new ecological reality will, in Latouche's estimation, require the 'decolonisation of the imaginary' and by implication, a new, raised political awareness and consciousness.

Latouche acknowledges that the alternatives to expansionist growth are potentially present at the individual, local community, regional, national and global levels of society. But when faced with an anti-democratic, tyranny of the 'new masters of the universe' more democratic levers of power will have to be found to organise in a 'concerted and complementary fashion'. (Latouche, P. 68) Latouche goes on to present a very practical electoral programme which under the present neo-liberal economic regime would prove difficult to deliver. Latouche is under no illusions about enacting the policies he advocates, "The implementation of realistic and rational proposals has little chance of being adopted and still less chance of succeeding unless the entire system is subverted."

(Latouche, P.76) He goes on to argue for the possibility for a 'gentle transition' through a gradual approach but accepts that preconditions have to be created in order to effect a radical change in direction. Latouche, however, is very aware that to subvert the capitalist order would challenge its basic foundation, the 'private ownership of the means of production' and 'would plunge society into chaos' without abolishing 'the capitalist imaginary' or 'spirit' of capitalism which he views as the psychological mindset to be rooted out.

Latouche makes clear that de-growth is not a call to return to a romantic nostalgic past nor to try and civilize and put a human face on capitalism. In advocating going beyond post industrial society and the reasons for it, he quotes Murray Bookchin's comment that, "Capitalism can no more be 'persuaded' to limit growth than a human being can be 'persuaded' to stop breathing." (Latouche, P. 90) However, historically, societies have accepted and functioned with private ownership, money, wage relationships and even capitalists since, "those 'economic' relations do not dominate either the production or circulation of 'goods and services'...They are neither market societies, wage-based societies nor industrial societies, and still less are they capitalist societies, even though both capital and capitalists can be found in them." (Latouche,P. 91/92) He, therefore, does not advocate getting rid of currencies, markets, financial and industrial profits, but 'it means embedding them in a different logic' and that is what a shift from the Newtonian to the quantum paradigm would, over time, achieve. The most sure way to decolonise the mindset associated with the 'spirit' of capitalism is to demonstrate the scientific, quantum foundation for the evolution of an incontrovertible, ecological and ethical logic in which humanity would be embedded in the rhythms, cycles and interdependencies of nature itself. De-growth is in essence, a humanist project involving what Latouche refers to as 'a re-enchantment of the world', to offset the 'banal commodification' of life in an alienated, commercialized and conditioned social landscape, where art and artists endeavour to remind us, that we too can be creators and bring shared values and meaning to human existence. But in order to challenge the 'spirit' of capitalism and replace it with a new creative, re-enchanted spirit, broader and more humane, will require a fundamental change in our individual awareness, collective consciousness and ethical codes of behaviour, in tune with the potential inherent in the discoveries of ecological biology and the paradoxes of quantum science itself.

11 EVOLUTION OF CONSCIOUSNESS

A growing number of cultural thinkers now fervently proclaim that humanity is at a crossroads in its evolutionary journey, a journey that is both potentially dangerous and awe inspiring in its possibilities. At this juncture, it is important to perceive what is substantive and superficial and know what, in our culture, is being born and what is dying. The human psyche or consciousness is gradually being influenced by the unifying revelations of quantum physics, 'spiritual' awakening and the transformation of our world view into one which embraces a visionary, ecological wholeness. This outlook contrasts with a deeply felt consensual absence of any collective meaning to life, combined with a cynical pessimism, alienation and hedonistic nihilism, so prevalent in the Western world today. This distorted world view has evolved under the powerful influence of scientific materialism, an off shoot of the Newtonian paradigm and its mechanistic, reductionist methodologies which analyse the parts to the detriment of understanding the whole.

A common analogy or literary device can be used to describe the evolution of humanity through the growth and development of an individual human being from childhood, through the stormy years of adolescence to adult maturity. Deeply embedded in our view of human evolution is the general assumption that aggressiveness, competitiveness and selfishness are integral aspects of human nature, pre-determined by our 'selfish genes', which can be managed and controlled but not eradicated. According to cultural historian, Lewis Mumford, "What is conspicuous in neolithic diggings... is the complete absence of weapons." Confirming these findings for the Paleolithic age, the archaeologist, W.J. Perry states that, "It is an error as profound as it is universal, to think that men in the food gathering stage were given to fighting....The study of the Paleolithic age fails to reveal any definite signs of human warfare."(Quoted in Sacred Eyes, L. Robert Keck,1992, P.34) The values thus derived from such a 'childhood' lived in close proximity to nature. Its symbolic figurines of the mother, goddess and feminine, suggest a cultural and ecological respect for nature governed by a feminine principle which encouraged sexual equality amidst a nurturing, relatively peaceful, cooperative existence.

The further evolution of humanity, like our own adolescence, was a natural search for a sense of self identity and independence through ego and mental maturation. This manifested in our separation from nature around 8,000 BC. when we began to control and manipulate nature in the belief that we stood above nature and given 'dominion' over it by religious authority. Though a necessary part of our evolution, the more complex society became, the more separation manifested itself through categorization, compartmentalisation, distinction and division leading to further disconnections from nature and a sense of wholeness. Out of this growing separation from nature and each other came the dominant values of our evolutionary 'adolescence'; hierarchy, patriarchy, power and authority. These elitist categories were encompassed within societies that around 4,500 BC were becoming more restless,violent and warring and ruled by priests and warriors who had replaced the feminine Goddess with masculine Gods. Archaeological digs reveal major migrations of dislocation and destruction which apparently avoided isolated Agean islands like Crete, Thera and Malta until around 1500. BC

At this time, in early human 'adolescent' maturation, a collective consciousness emerged across many cultures which manifested in creation myths. These myths spoke to a sense of loss, of humanity's 'Fall', not down, but up into a new ego-consciousness of separation. The Judeo-Christian, Garden of Eden is the dominant Western myth. Creation myths are similar around the world; everywhere, a memory of an idyllic past or 'childhood' followed by a dramatic transition to an egoic 'adolescent' consciousness accompanied by the retreat from nurturing Goddess cultures to dominant masculine God cultures. Early Christianity cultivated a variety of theological values and a more balanced judgement regarding females acting as priests and carrying out spiritual functions until prominent theological Fathers, like Irenaeus and Tertullian, expressed a distinct dislike for women acting in church roles, thus undermining their spiritual authority and establishing patriarchy as the dominant ethos.

The umbilical cord, with nature and the feminine principle, was cut and 'civilisation' arose. According to cultural historian, William Irvin Thompson," Mesolithic society may have seen the domestication of animals, and Neolithic society may have seen the domestication of plants, but what the age after the neolithic sees is the domestication of women by men." (quoted in 'Sacred Eyes', L.Robert Keck P.44.) Here, myths reveal themselves, not as fantasies, but revelations of the emergence of a new level of human consciousness and sense of self- awareness and individual independence. This view, of course, can be contrasted with the traditional religious interpretation of the 'Fall' as the 'depravity of humanity' caused by increasing knowledge and man's disobedience to God, then seen as the 'original sin'. It was, therefore, from the values inherent in the religious perspective, mainly the Judeo-Christian and Islamic monotheistic spiritual traditions, that we view the first years of our 'adolescent' existence. These years witnessed the evolution of patriarchy, hierarchical power, belief systems, conformist authority and often pathological violence.

One of the most potent myth's in the transformation from humanity's subconscious embrace with the 'Great Mother', is the myth of the 'hero' and his heroic slaying of the of the 'Dragon'.

"Somewhere during this period, the Hero clutched his egoic self out of the jaws of the Devouring Mother and secured his own emancipation.... But in its zeal to assert its independence, it not only transcended the Great Mother, which was desirable; it repressed the Great Mother, which was disastrous. And there the ego - the Western ego - demonstrated not just an awakened assertiveness, but a blind arrogance." (Up From Eden, Ken Wilbur, 1981, P. 193 & 195). The fledgling ego thus turned its own transcendence and differentiation from nature into repression, dissociation and ultimately alienation from her nurturing presence, sense of wholeness and potential for wholesome living. However, behind the dissolution of the bond between humanity and nature was a social and technological transformation which dissolved this association and launched mankind in a new, uncertain direction, a quest to discover himself.

Unlike the shamanism associated with the natural spirituality of our 'childhood ', early 'adolescence' was consumed with the rise of religions which sought an ultimate power, external to humanity. This evolved into institutionalised religion which required intermediaries to interpret belief, ritual and behaviour in line with the power of a priesthood. It was during Medieval times that witnessed the ultimate authority of the church, the power of patriarchy, and violence against women in witch-hunts. "The adolescent propensity for an unbalanced masculinity, violence, simplistic belief systems, and immaturity reached pathological proportions and gruesome manifestations in the Middle Ages." (Sacred Eyes, P.53) It was through the priesthood's intercessions with the external divine that their authority was derived and control maintained. These comments, it should be stressed, are not arguments against Christianity but the way in which humanity in its early immature 'adolescence' interpreted Christ's mission. Instead of seeing him as 'one of us', a 'spiritual guide', a representation of what humanity could become in its maturity, as the 'heretical' Gnostic Gospels had pronounced, his role was interpreted, as with God, a divine power outside the literal reach of humanity. And so was born a 'heroic' divinity, a role which was embellished in the New Testament.

The 14th to the 17th centuries represented a transition from viewing the world through the religious eyes of early 'adolescence' to seeing the world through the scientific lens of late 'adolescence'. The period included violent purges associated with

Jewish pogroms, the helplessness experienced during the Black Death, the scientific revelations of Kepler, Bruno and Galileo, and the corruption of the Catholic Church, culminating in the Protestant Reformation. According to Rupert Sheldrake, "The Protestants were trying to bring about an irreversible change in attitude, eradicating the traditional idea that spiritual power pervades the natural world,....The Reformation thus prepared the ground for the mechanistic revolution in science....Nature was already disenchanted and the material world separated from the life of the spirit; the idea that the universe was merely a vast machine fitted well with this kind of theology,....The domains of science and religion could now be separated: science taking the whole of nature for its province, including the human body; and religion the moral and spiritual aspects of the human soul." (The Rebirth of Nature: The Greening of Science and God, Rupert Sheldrake, 1990, P. 20/21)

Unfortunately, we may have changed the lens but continued using the same 'adolescent' value system and its concomitant egotistical behaviour. As early 'adolescence' sought an external religious 'saviour', late 'adolescent' humanity, through science, sought to gain more power over nature and institute a scientific system commensurate with the 'adolescent' need for patriarchal control. In humanity's inherent quest for truth and meaning it evolved from the worship of God and the Medieval church to the worship of science's capacity to explain and make sense of the material world. In due course, especially after the accumulated discoveries of Kepler and Galileo, the philosophies of Bacon and Descartes to the ground breaking mathematics of Isaac Newton, science evolved into the dominant paradigm of the modern world, extolling the virtues of objectivity, rationalism and empiricism. As William Irvin Thompson remarks, "It was no longer a question of believing, but knowing, and.... scientists in their new ways of knowing the world succeeded in taking charisma away from the Church" (quoted in Sacred Eyes, P.60), and in the process a scientific priesthood arose armed with a specialised knowledge and language, which,in time, became the primary authority, an elite among other lesser elites. During this transition, questions of meaning, related to the 'why' of things were reduced to questions of 'what' and 'how' making scientific materialism, the 'religion' of our time and almost heretical to challenge its basic assumptions.

Although we have progressed in evolutionary terms from early 'adolescence', our late 'adolescent' values and behaviour remained immature. This again, is not an argument against science as a method of evidence based enquiry but a riposte to upholding scientific materialism as the only way to truth, a way in which some scientists believe has turned science into a dogma. While Bacon's legacy justified the 'rape' of nature in its feminist form for human benefit and Descartes split mind from body and matter from spirit, Newton transformed it into a cosmic machine. Here, Carolyn Merchant comments on the key philosophical and practical significance of the 'death of nature' through the Scientific Revolution. "Because nature was now viewed as a system of dead, inert particles moved by external, rather than inherent forces, the mechanical framework itself could legitimate the manipulation of nature." (Quoted in Sacred Eyes, P. 63)

The eminent biologist, Rupert Sheldrake, has challenged the dogmatic basis on which modern science rests. He is convinced that, "The biggest scientific delusion of all is that science already knows the answers. The details still need working out but, in principle, the fundamental questions are settled. Contemporary science is based on the claim that all reality is material or physical. There is no reality but material reality. Consciousness is a by-product of the physical activity of the brain. Matter is unconscious. Evolution is purposeless. These beliefs are powerful,…The facts of science are real enough; so are the techniques that scientists use, and the technologies based on them. But the belief system that governs conventional scientific thinking is an act of faith, grounded in a nineteenth-century ideology." (The Science Delusion: Freeing the Spirit of Enquiry, Rupert Sheldrake. 2012, P. 6/7) His book goes on to challenge ten core beliefs of contemporary science of which two are very pertinent to our subject matter, that is, the mechanical nature of life and that all matter is unconscious and that human consciousness is simply a product of the material brain. Sheldrake emphasises that the world view of scientific materialism, despite all the advances in science and technology, "is now facing a credibility crunch that was unimaginable in the 20th century." (Sheldrake, P.9) The above two key issues in biology, development and consciousness, remain unresolved, despite the attempts of Francis Crick and Sydney Brenner, both ardent materialists, who were determined to show that physics and chemistry alone would prove the material basis of life.

It would appear that the evolution of our late 'adolescent' consciousness has got stuck in the 'matter' from which it initially emerged from. It might be deduced from scientific materialism that humanity has reached the pinnacle of evolutionary development and consciousness; a consciousness still rooted in the 19th century idea of unlimited material 'progress'. It would seem that scientific materialism has engineered a scientific, technological economy to satisfy all our psychological and physical needs, and consumer desires, but for all its wizardry remains blinkered or blind to the growing evidence of the multi-dimensional crisis we are presently facing. In our late 'adolescence', western science gave life to scientific materialism, which, in its egoic arrogance has reduced its perception of life to a machine while capitalist culture has turned our economies into social injustice, inequality and institutionalised greed; our politics into bureaucracy and expediency; our democracy into elitism and disillusionment; our values into acquisitive consumption, nihilism and hedonism and our psyches into fragmented personalities, insecurity and fear of the future.

There are a growing number of prophetic voices who contend that this egoic description is simply, metaphorically speaking, evidence of humanity's evolving maturation from an 'adolescent,' 'dark night of the human soul', to adulthood and subsequently, a higher level of development and consciousness. These voices range from social analysts like Alvin Toffler, economists like Paul Hawken, paleontologists like Teilhard de Chardin, physicists like John Platt, and historians like Theodore Roszak, all of whom perceive that humanity is undergoing a radical historical and cultural transformation. If we dare listen to these voices they will tell us that as the butterfly struggles to metamorphose from the caterpillar our civilisation may be confronted with the traumas associated with a transition fraught with uncertainty, fear and insecurity. Thus levels of disorganisation, destruction and breakdown – which we are experiencing at this moment - may precede reintegration, restructuring and eventual breakthrough. This duality has always been part of human evolutionary transformation. However, with growth in our awareness, as rapid as the speed of contemporary change in online and social media technologies, the transition - although generational in time scale - may not be as traumatic or as slow as we might think. At the same time, we can be inspired by the possibilities opened up by the now scientifically established, conceptual framework of quantum physics. Its dynamic principles of unity, integration and interdependence could lay the foundations upon which mature human 'adulthood' values and behaviour could emerge. All of these principles are inherent processes that have the power to create a higher level of individual and collective consciousness capable of shifting hardened mindsets, dogmatic attitudes, flawed perceptions, acquisitive compulsions and corrupted values.

The belief espoused here is that a growth in awareness and consciousness is integral to human evolutionary transformation and cannot be stunted or arrested in any phase of human development. The present and forthcoming transformation will favour transcendence to a higher level of human well being and 'quality of life', spiritual as well as material. However, before becoming over optimistic about the nature of this transformation we ought to consider the question of the all pervading global, negative 'social mood' of the present time. According to Bill Harris and other commentators, positive and negative social moods related to 'good' or 'bad' times become fairly accurate, predictable indicators of the degree of social turmoil that may be experienced before emerging into more calm social waters. In an article entitled, 'Going to Hell in a Handbasket, Part 1' he comments, " I do see us entering such a time of increasingly negative social mood – in fact a big one. And though things are obviously much more contentious and negative now than they were ten years ago (or even five) I don't think the real dark times are here yet. When such times come, human beings can do such savage things that its almost unbelievable. The 1930's and 1940's provide the most recent relative big example!... When times of social mood come, civilisation flies out of the window, and it will this time too." (Centerpointe Research Institute, Bill Harris, Feb. 22nd 2011) The surprising aspect of this comment is that it was made by the director of an organisation that promotes courses in meditation and well-being, guided by spiritual values to encourage growth in awareness and consciousness. Since this is a global transformation we are presently transiting, the volcanic eruption of the 'Arab Spring', revolts in Greece, and mass demonstrations in Spain, Brazil and elsewhere confirms that radical change has often to be paid for in human lives, especially when hardened dictatorships and authoritarian governments resist popular pressure for greater levels of equality, justice and democracy.

PART THREE

12 THE PARTICIPATORY UNIVERSE

Crucial to this transformational paradigm is the conscious spread of the unifying principles associated with quantum science regarding the potential for the growth of human awareness and consciousness. The complementarity principle – whereby the quantum wave collapses to the quantum particle under experimental observation - demonstrates the potential power of human observation and consciousness in influencing material reality. The physicist, John Wheeler, highlights the philosophic and human implications of the respected, but still controversial, Copenhagen interpretation of quantum physics; "The universe does not exist 'out there', independent of us. We are inescapably involved in bringing about that which appears to be happening. We are not only observers. We are participators. In some strange sense this is a participatory universe." (quoted in 'Whole in One', by David Lorimer, 1990, P. 261) The 'non-local', interdependency principle of quantum reality is spelt out by Fritjof Capra, "These non-local connections are the essence of quantum reality. Each event is influenced by the whole universe... Whereas the hidden variables in classical physics are local mechanisms, those in quantum physics are non-local; they are instantaneous connections to the whole universe." (The Turning Point, Fritjof Capra, P. 71)

It is on the basis of these and other quantum principles that the philosophy of 'deep ecology', its strategies and popular movement have evolved. We are faced with a seemingly insurmountable dilemma; an ecological crisis bordering on disaster; unlimited growth economies floundering blindly and overwhelmed by their own inner contradictions; societies whose social fabrics are torn apart by inequality, poverty and deprivation; ethnic and sectarian divisions; national and international crisis and wars; political structures that are growing in irrelevance; democracies that work for an elite few; materialistic, nihilistic, hedonistic and atomistic cultures purged of shared human moral and ethical values and compassion; and all of this, confronted by a sense of individual paralysis and impotence. This ecological, socio-economic and political crisis, and the personal powerlessness experienced in the face of it, are linked to a spiritual crisis. This is not like that experienced by institutionalised religion which is suffering its own but connected spiritual problems, but an overwhelming Western spiritual crisis that evokes a sense of personal and cultural emptiness, devoid of meaning, purpose. belonging and vision. "We face a spiritual crisis not just because we have a less easy faith in the old gods and the old, established religions, but because, with this, we have lost our sense of what it is to be human....we need the transforming vision to see that....the deepest roots of our humanity are to be found within the wider natural world. We need to recapture the natural within ourselves, and to see that within such natural rootedness lies our empowerment to act." (The Quantum Society, Dana Zohar & Ian Marshall, P. 181/182)

Modern rationality and reason which culminated in the European Enlightenment, has, under the weight of the old scientific paradigm, been reduced to 'instrumental reason'. Although it has created many benefits which freed us from some of nature's limitations, it has, nevertheless, produced mind numbing, bureaucratic and impersonal, Kafkaesque institutions and organisations which treat human beings like objects, machine like parts for manipulation and use. In the end, reason, truth and science have become instruments of power, and paradoxically, shut down our faith in rationality and hope in our future. Our separation from nature or Gaia, literally, the body that gave humanity its birth, and so revered by ancient cultures, is the genesis of our spiritual predicament. The Oxford philosopher, John Gray comments here on the depth of the spiritual crisis we are facing, "I want to argue that we could not respond positively and creatively to the now desperate state of our environment from within the old Western world view, be that Christian, humanist or mechanistic." (quoted in The Quantum Society, P. 188).

Looking beyond the Newtonian paradigm towards the quantum world view we find a number of controversial approaches to this crisis. There are councils of despair adopted by cynics of all persuasions who feel that we have no power to act. The various green schools of eco-philosophy compete with each other rather than integrate their ideas and energies in a united challenge to the present anthropocentric, corporate culture. Nostalgic romantics spiral us back to traditional rural communities devoid of all the scientific and technological benefits reaped from the positive advances made through Newtonian science. On the other hand, the quantum world view combined with deep ecological awareness encourages an upward spiral of hope where human beings are valued as integral to the all embracing, earth centred processes of the natural world. "The quantum world view is, in its very essence, an ecological world view. But it rests on an ecological vision that can use rather than abandon science and technology, a vision that expands the foundations of human reason rather than undermining or limiting them. And it is a vision that takes us forward from where we are now, using the best of all we have achieved while relinquishing the attitudes that have made these achievements destructive." (The Quantum Society, P. 189)

The quantum 'complementarity' principle has undermined the false division between humanity and the natural world. As observers we can no longer view nature as an object to be manipulated and exploited for ends that no longer serve genuine, humane purposes, but as an integral part of our own body, mind and spirit. If we live in what John Wheeler calls a 'participatory universe' we have the power to bring forth a world of our own creative imagination which would offer us insightful ways in the use of technology and an economy for sound, ecologically sustainable ends. Another relationship between the observer and the observed, is at the moment speculative, but nevertheless profound in its implications. It is the belief "that the nature of mind, the nature of society and the nature of nature are all one and the same thing, that all are linked by a common physics,..." (The Quantum Society, P. 190) This speculative, but inherently logical conclusion provides an added strength to the efficacy of deep ecology as the over-arching imperative for our survival and empowerment to act.

Nature, from this perspective has been deeply felt through the experience of the 'wisdom traditions' of native cultures for millennia. Here, Chief Seattle encapsulates a whole natural philosophy in a few simple words, "Whatever befalls the earth, befalls the sons and daughters of the earth. Man did not weave the web of life; he is merely a strand in it. Whatever he does to the web, he does to himself." (Chief Seattle, Quoted in, The Web of Life,F Capra) Jimmy Reid said something similar, in equally simple language, "Break one link in the chain and we might rue the consequences. Break many links and we might die from the consequences. Man's dominion over his fellow creatures should never be arrogantly discharged. We are part of nature's overall equation, not above or beyond it....The human species can do anything within the laws of nature. When we try to work out with these laws we are in danger, even if we don't yet know the essence of the dangers." (Jimmy Reid, Choked By Our Own Greed, in Power Without Principles, 1999, P. 84) Through the quantum, ecological world view humanity is in the process of maturing to its 'adult' stage of evolutionary consciousness from where we can develop a new, more inspired and responsible relationship with nature and with each other. As an integral part of nature we have been given the responsibility as 'humble servants' to recreate a world in tune with the principles of quantum, ecological reality which fundamentally challenges the arrogant sentiments of the old paradigm, that we are the end for which all else was created. In this sense, "To be good citizens, to become what Richard Falk calls 'citizen pilgrims', we must embed all these feelings and insights in political action. We must engage ourselves actively and directly in resistance to the social and political ills we see around us. We must, as Falk says, be willing to 'get our hands dirty'." (The Quantum Society, P.200/201)

13 DEMOCRACY INVERTED

Before we can take effective political action in transforming societies from human centred to earth centred we have first to acknowledge the way in which democratic institutions have been corrupted and weakened over the last three or more decades. In essence, with honourable exceptions, it is a failure of political will by a political 'class' that has been corrupted by its ascendancy into the higher echelons of elitist society and close personal and psychological proximity to those who wield wealth and economic power, combined with its estrangement from the people whose trust they have diluted for personal or ideological reasons. The powerful rule through the passivity of the electorate and very rarely look over their shoulder at the peoples displeasure with their performance or policies. The growing realisation that it is transnational corporations, as opposed to popular will, that sets the global economic agenda is awakening people to the necessity of recapturing the levers of democratic legitimacy. "For democracy to flourish, we need our own moment of admission that our economic system has failed... we also need to take a long hard look not only at the free market but at the political system that supports it. It's in reclaiming the idea that we're able to think for ourselves and that we are ready for politics, rather than outsourcing it like so much else, that we will be able to reclaim both democracy and our economy." (The Value of Nothing, How to Reshape Market Society and Redefine Democracy, Raj Patel, 2009, P. 119)

Politicians, especially 'career' politicians, have become a 'caste apart' which corrupts the basic principle of representative government. Obama's campaign cry, 'No more politics as usual' resonated around the world but sadly to little effect when he came to power where the corporate agenda was still set by Wall Street power brokers. Popular movements, like Green Peace, or anyone who protests against the ideological, Washington consensus are deemed threats to the state and depending upon where this 'threat' is located in the world will be branded as either terrorists, criminals, urban hooligans or dissidents. 'Democracies' that cannot tolerate dissidents who express legitimate grievances associated with economic and political institutions that have apparently become 'incorporated' into the dominant neo-liberal ideology are defective, not only in democratic credentials, but open to Bertolt Brecht's anti-fascist warning, that 'the beast is still on heat'.

Sheldon Wolin's book, 'Democracy Incorporated:Managed Democracy and the Specter of Inverted Totalitarianism' is a study of the demise of democracy in America and its 'totalitarian' implications. From the outset he makes it abundantly clear that he doesn't compare America with the 'classic' totalitarian states of Nazi Germany, Italian fascism or the communist Soviet Union. He does, however, show that totalitarian states can and do take different forms. Thus in contrast to classic totalitarianism, "...inverted totalitarianism is only in part a state centered phenomenon. Primarily it represents the political coming of age of corporate power and the political demobilisation of the citizenry." (Democracy Incorporated:Managed Democracy and the Specter of Inverted Totalitarianism, Sheldon Wolin, 2008, Preface, xviii) Inverted totalitarianism is a far cry from Adam Smith's, 'unseen hand' upon which the market operated on a decentralised principle for everyone's self-interested benefit. The growth of big business and ultimately the corporation, reinforced by social Darwinism's 'survival of the fittest' mind-set, concentrated corporate and political power in a seemingly unassailable embrace, all to the detriment of democracy. Wolin argues that his term, 'inverted totalitarianism' is at present only a possible hypothesis but he is, "convinced that certain tendencies in our society point in a direction away from self-government, the rule of law, egalitarianism, and thoughtful public discussion, and toward what I have called 'managed democracy,' the smiley face of inverted totalitarianism."....and warns whether,

"we want to exchange our birthrights for its mess of pottage."
(Wolin, Preface, xxiv)

Although Wolin's study is focused on America we can see similar elements of democracy's demise across the Western world. Managed democracy is not neutral. It takes its lead from the culture of business, which, spurred on by the neo-liberal economy pushes legal and ethical limits in ways that are indisputably criminal. Corporate power extends its tentacles through the exchange of personnel from corporations to military and government office and promotes privatisation as the legitimate expression of electoral will at the expense of welfare programmes. All of these corporate interventions with political obeisance have the accumulative affect of acclimatising and disciplining the public in acquiring behaviours of submission and acquiescence to ruling elites. The sum and substance of this insidious encroachment on hard won democratic rights is that, "The union of corporate and state power means that, instead of the illusion of a leaner system of governance, we have the reality of a more extensive, more invasive system than ever before, one removed from democratic influences and hence better able to manage democracy." (Wolin, P. 137)

The 21st century is not facing a 'brave new world' of economic progress, supported by scientific wizardry and technological fixes but a nightmarish world of increasing conflict, hierarchical and oligarchic power free from democratic control and accountability. Traditionally, the democratic political ideal espoused an ethos of cultivating cooperative arrangements, whereby the people expressed a shared belief in the way power was 'gifted' to their political representatives and the way in which this gift was ultimately accountable to them. In contrast, the corporate ethos is essentially anti-political and anti-democratic. Its culture is founded on a Darwinian, competitive behavioural pattern, which, metaphorically, can be likened to that of a shark, an animal that has to keep on the move to survive while periodically entering an acquisition frenzy when tearing another corporation apart to gain supremacy in stealing its markets, brand names and innovative technology. This kind of rapacious behaviour confirms the way Enron operated, and no doubt many other corporations. Enron's chief financial officer's, 'vision and values' sign on display read, "When Enron says it will rip your face off, it will rip your face off." (quoted in Wolin, P.138) It is clear, that driven by excess profitability, operational ruthlessness and the inherent compulsion to expand, the larger society - which it is dependent upon to produce and consume its products - is reduced in the main to servile labour, harsh working conditions, low wages, union discouragement and job insecurity, the severity of which, being all dependent on where in the world the corporation is operating from.

Wolin gives Wal-Mart as an example of the 'aggrandizing culture' of the corporation and its 'invasive, totalizing power' which has the capability of damaging whole communities including small local businesses. We can see these same effects when Tesco comes to town. But none of this could happen without the collusion of local politicians. Allied with an 'aggrandizing culture' comes an almost untouchable corporate 'criminal culture'. Corporate crimes committed by corporation executives are on the increase. The cheating, deceit and fraud are symptomatic of the degree by which corporations have been 'liberated' from any pretence at government regulation. Schumpeter coined the phrase, 'creative destructiveness' in reference to the positive and negative effects of capitalist practice. Just as a military conflict produces 'collateral damage', 'downsizing' is the corporate equivalent in their drive to remain competitive. The economic casualties, in this case, are destroyed careers, lives disrupted and hopes smashed. In the political arena, the collateral damage is the sacrificing of the poor and deprived through the attacks on welfare benefits, minimum wages, health and safety standards, short working contracts, employment blacklists and general material and psychological insecurity. Relative inequality is now prevalent across the whole world. It has now been estimated that three hundred people own more wealth than three billion citizens. The collateral damage from both the corporate and political domains is having a destructive effect on the once secure traditional middle classes. Wolin's statement here could equally be applied to Britain and Europe, "A government responsive to the deepening distress of the Many, to ever widening class disparities, to impending environmental crisis, would need sufficient autonomy to defy corporate wishes. The fact that government rarely challenges corporate power allows capital to define the political terrain to fit its own needs." (Wolin, P. 144)

It is evident from the all prevailing neo-liberal consensus that Friedmanite principles are now deeply ingrained in Western culture. Their influence stretches from the economics classrooms in the topmost respected Universities of the West, down to aggressive TV games like 'The Apprentice' where the Trumps and Sugars of this world pedal their nostrums about business values, managerial practice and appropriate competitive behaviour, which in essence can all be reduced to a 'dog eat dog' mindset. This is, 'creative' capitalism at work, a world that is today revered by the corporate and political elites of Western civilisation and generally acquiesced in by the 'common' people. This is the cold, calculating, neo-liberal, monolithic machine promoted by the economic philosophies of Hayek and Friedman and given birth to by cutting edge, political midwives like Pinochet, Xiaoping, Thatcher and Reagan who socially engineered their societies in the image of unfettered, corporate capitalism. Using measures such as council house purchase and opportunities to invest in public utilities, Mrs Thatcher seduced the general population into believing that all in society could be an investor, property owner or potential capitalist - the latter day 'American Dream'.

With out doubt, Thatcherism, released an energy so powerful in its long term effects that it fundamentally transformed the collective consciousness of Britain. So much so, that all governments that followed - including Blair's, Brown's and Cameron's coalition government - adhered to the same Thatcherite principles. In a prophetic statement on the political and economic influence of Mrs Thatcher, Jimmy Reid had this to say, "My fear for my country is that it is being governed by a woman who seems utterly devoid of compassion. Thatcher is dangerous because she is absolutely certain she is right about absolutely everything. Her mind appears closed to the slightest possibility that she might ever be wrong. Another five years of Thatcherism could be a disaster and could destroy all the social achievements of a century of struggle by decent men and women." (Daily Record, 14th March 1983, As I Please, 1984, P. 29) If Jimmy Reid could testify to Mrs Thatcher's influence over five years, her ideological impact over the time she took office and the emulating governments that followed, are socially, economically and politically incalculable. This is the mountain the opposition to neo-liberal capitalism have to climb in Britain and it is even higher and harder to climb in America where the constitutional arrangements have been for a long time deliberately engineered, so that, "the electoral system could be stacked so as to prevent its being used to promote a populist agenda, and no where more clearly than in the provision governing the most crucial power a democracy can have, the power to change its constitution." (Wolin, P. 155)

The neo-liberal consensus will be difficult and even hazardous to transform given the collusion between the state and global capitalism. It will be doubly difficult given the prevailing cynicism, lethargy, apathy, and alienation of the electorate, what Wolin refers to as 'Civic demobilisation', a conditioning that stimulates a little interest during elections followed by immersion in consumer distractions, media frippery and personal interests. These distractions need not be politically or socially engineered. When combined with the current high-tech pace of life, long working hours, short term contracts, job insecurity and a general collective uncertainty and fear for the future, it all takes its toll on people's motivation and willpower to participate in what the majority feel is a pointless and powerless exercise. What we have generally in the West now are powerful states and failing, participatory democracies. The dumbing down of public debate on the key issue of corporate hegemony, the challenges of failing American imperial and economic power and the ritualistic, celebratory forms of post-imperial Britain, all contribute to the reality, whereby politically managed democratic forms take precedence over democratic substance. Thus, " In the face of declining political involvement by ordinary citizens, democracy becomes dangerously empty and not only receptive to anti-political appeals to blind patriotism, fear, and demagoguery but comfortable with a political culture where lying, misrepresentation, and deception have become normal practice."(Wolin, P.261)

It is clear from the above that the problem of rolling back managerial, 'inverted', democracy and reviving the essence of democratic practice is one of the major challenges for the future. The attempt to install a genuine participatory democracy within a corporate state locked into the all pervading ideological consensus of global, neo-liberal capitalism is much more than a challenge. In the absence of an egalitarian vision which emphasises the commonality and equality of humanity as the foundation for fundamental change, will make this challenge extremely difficult indeed. Our democracies came into being after a long and hard struggle by the 'common' people. Capitalism evolved to satisfy the interests of the 'bourgeoisie' who created economic principles, institutions and practices to conform with their conception of individual liberty, which in essence, guaranteed the sanctity, protection and ownership of private property. Deep ecology, along with other green and socialist economic philosophies criticise this interpretation of individual liberty. Perhaps a necessity in its day for promoting economic progress and development, but in its neo-liberal, predatory disguise places severe limitations on participatory, democratic liberty and has become an albatross around the neck of humanity. There are, however, many concepts of justice and rights. The dominant contemporary one being that which defends and secures the freedoms and rights of global capitalism to accumulate and expand through the mechanisms of market exchange. But, " However much we might wish rights to be universal, it is the state that has to enforce them. If political power is not willing, then notions of rights remain empty." (A Brief History of Neoliberalism, David Harvey, 2005, P. 180) If society wishes to challenge the dominance of these rights it will have to challenge the corporate state and all the traditional legal rights and ingrained assumptions that give it sustenance. There are, of course, many rights and freedoms, such as equal opportunity before the law, freedom of choice, freedom to contract and sell one's labour, freedom of thought, speech and expression being among the most important.

We have all probably experienced the flexibility of these laws and rights when confronted by powers in whose interest it is to get a favourable outcome. As David Harvey makes clear, " These derivative rights are appealing. Many of us rely heavily upon them. But we do so much as beggars live off the crumbs from the rich man's table. I cannot convince anyone by philosophical argument that the neoliberal regime of rights is unjust. But the objection to this regime of rights is quite simple: to accept it is to accept that we have no alternative except to live under a regime of endless capital accumulation and economic growth no matter what the social, ecological, or political consequences. Reciprocally, endless capital accumulation implies that the neoliberal regime of rights must be geographically expanded across the globe by violence (as in Chile and Iraq) by imperialist practices (such as those of the World Trade Organization, the IMF, and the World Bank)... By hook or by crook, the inalienable rights of private property and the profit rate will be universally established." (David Harvey, P. 181/182)

The UN Charter extols rights that go beyond the rights of the European and American revolutions which established the legality of capitalist accumulation and imperial expansion. They include the right to education and economic security, union organisation, freedom of speech and expression, freedom from child labour and exploitation. But in a world governed by the neo-liberal consensus and generally unenforced, these rights are blowing in the winds. If UN rights were enforced and given primacy over the sanctified rights to corporation property and the free market, it would pose a fundamental challenge to the hegemony of global capitalism. However, the UN is constituted to take its orders from the very states that enforce the neo-liberal consensus and its Charter can be ignored when its directives run contrary to big state policies as was the case over Iraq. The fact remains, neo-liberal influence in the Western world in particular, now extends over all the major international institutions, financial centres, banks, academic schools, think tanks and not least, government policies of whatever hue; even tighter than the Maffia's grip over city districts in New York in the hey day of prohibition and the mysterious Gatsby. Indeed, today there are Gatsbys' whose wealth would make the original Gatsby appear a pauper and whose oligarchic power has enabled them to accrue this wealth through mysterious tax evasion methods and international hideaways; all – despite ostensible efforts to clamp down on these practices - 'legitimised' by governments who ostensibly represent the people. As long as corporations exist in their present form they will continue to evade and avoid paying their share of taxes, despite government efforts to assuage public concerns.

Neo-liberalism is, paradoxically, the 'flowering' of the capitalist phase of humanity's long 'adolescence'. It is a 'coming of age', the most extreme expression of capitalism's individualistic, aggressive and egotistical tendencies which have created the illusion of our separation from nature, from each other, of matter from spirit, of parts from wholes. As the transformation of the Quantum paradigm proceeds and the levels of awareness and consciousness rise, individuals will come to realise their responsibility to the common good and commit themselves to a new reality and mindset. In fact, when we come to look at current developments in Latin America this awareness is already on the rise. As Wolin states, "...the democratization of politics remains merely formal without the democratization of the self. Democratization is not about being 'left alone.' but about becoming a self that sees the values of common involvements and endeavours and finds in them a source of self- fulfilment. Transformation is not a rarity but happens all the time..." (Wolin, P.289)

Jimmy Reid expressed this sentiment in a more passionate way, " To unleash the latent potential of our people requires that we give them responsibility. The untapped resources of the North Sea are as nothing compared to the untapped resources of our people, I am convinced that the great mass of our people go through life without a glimmer of what they could have contributed to their fellow human beings. This is a personal tragedy. It's a social crime. The flowering of each individual's personality and talents is the pre-condition for everyone's development." (The Glasgow Rectorial Address, Jimmy Reid, 1972)

The democratization of the self, like all social change in the past, depends on raising individual consciousness followed by commitment and participation in common struggle against injustice. Paulo Freire in his ground breaking work in raising levels of awareness through literacy and radical adult education in Brazil, called it 'the conscientization process.' " Freire's central theme is the revolutionary transformation of men's consciousness... through releasing the potential for action.... The great dilemma confronting mankind lies in choosing between the humanization or dehumanization of man." (The Concept of Radical Adult Education with Particular Reference to Paula Freire, Ivan Illich and the Third World, Bob Reid, in Essays in Adult Learning and Teaching, Manchester University,1984, P.37/38) Freire goes on to explain that the poor and oppressed in identifying with their oppressors develop an inauthentic self. This becomes, "....the central problem for Freires's pedagogy....According to Freire the answer lies in the oppressed first discovering that their consciousness is false. The second step lies in developing an independent authentic consciousness so that the oppressed come to recognise their own oppression." (Bob Reid, P37/38.) The West may be more sophisticated than the third world but Freire's principle of the existence of a conditioned, inauthentic self or false consciousness, which thwarts social change, is as relevant to the developed Western world as to the underdeveloped world.

The Enlightenment concept of individual liberty was appropriate for its time. It was a response to the tyrannies of absolute monarchies, established churches and aristocracies. It was
to free and empower individuals as the source of their own authority in matters of business, moral persuasion and spiritual
choice. But like so many established traditions this hard won
liberty has with time turned into its opposite, "The neutrality
of the public sphere was to turn back on that very same individual with a vengeance never foreseen when the liberal ideal got
turned on its head through the political and social side effects
of modernity and the mechanistic view." (Zohar & Marshall, P.
213) The social consequences of industrialisation and the accompanying concept of mechanism and population growth are,
'bigness, rationalism and bureaucracy.' As society grew more
complex, reason, applied to bureaucracy, was meant to do away
with injustices and corruption. This was to be an extension of
individual liberty but since bureaucracies can only deal with
issues of common concern and as bureaucracy grew, more and
more people became disenchanted and alienated, so much so,
that in personal terms, "Power and authority has slipped from
my grasp to reside in the neutral bureaucratic authority that
treats me as a replaceable part in the system. I am reduced,
dis-empowered. I am a number or a type or a stage in the process of production.... When this system is the political system
that runs my country, I feel alienated as a citizen....This is particularly true when the political system is embodied in professional politicians who are distant and who seem to have their
own agenda....the dream of the liberal Enlightenment has led in
the West to the nightmare of bureaucracy and its loss of meaning." (Zohar & Marshall, P. 215/216)

What has emerged is the 'organization man' who is governed
by and applies rules with the minimum of discretion which reduces personal concerns to a morality that is mechanistic and
legalistic. Where social and political meaning have been reduced
to personal interpretation and denied a healthy outlet, it may
take a pathological direction and expression in finding mean-

ing in the empty symbols of materialism, to bolster and raise self-esteem, provide identity or manifest in urban riots and criminal behaviour. Without shared values and public meaning society can drift into forms of 'tribalism' which exploits racial, ethnic, religious and class tensions in its twisted quest for meaning. Nationalism, in its militaristic and tribal disguise, has also the propensity to become a social pathology. When a large percentage of the electorate are disenchanted by the political process and society is riven with economic warfare reflecting the divide between those that hold wealth and power and those at the receiving end of injustice and inequality, the only result is to defend the interests of each group. " All this is of course made stronger still by the liberal democratic tradition that politics shall be a pursuit of interests, that I best serve democracy by best serving my own interests, and that it is healthy for different interests to oppose each other (the politics of adversarial democracy). Faith in Adam Smith's 'invisible hand' has not been justified by results." (Zohar & Marshall, P. 222)

It is evident that seeking national or international consensus based on such adversarial politics and 'inverted' managerial democracy is problematic. A prolonged struggle will be necessary to establish a unifying ecological goal which has the earth's interest central to that goal. This does not mean the negation of democracy. Participatory democracy of a more meaningful kind will emerge to debate with passion with all those who have the earth's and humanity's interests at heart as to what policies, structures, strategies and intermediate goals are best pursued for the common good. This process will offer authentic voices and choices as opposed to one choice before us at present; the corporate state and managed democracy - take it or leave it! This negative choice has allowed economic, political and unethical exploitation, assisted by authoritarian and right wing governments, to spread their tentacles further and deeper into our lives and consciousness.

During the 1930's depression President Roosevelt made it clear that 'excessive profits' and 'undue private power' were its cause and proclaimed an alternative vision of rights and obligations. The state, including civil society, was obliged to vanquish poverty and give security and safeguards against the often harsh circumstances of life, which, along with decent housing would ensure freedom from want. This contrasts with the narrow inverted freedoms offered by Presidents Reagan and Bush who extolled the virtues of deregulated free market enterprise, the withdrawal of the state from welfare provision and the fostering of all 'freedoms' to extend the influence of neo-liberal power. Due to the fact that there is very little debate regarding the appropriateness of neo-liberal notions of state obligations and freedoms gives the impression that there are no alternatives to this ideological doctrine. The 2008 financial crash combined with unethical corporation practices and their effect on the state, could never be compared to the morality and ethics expressed in either Marx's ideas on freedom or Adam Smith's 'Theory of Moral Sentiments', the very auricle the neo-liberal fraternity hold up as the god-father of laissez faire purity. By any analysis and measurement, the doctrine and practice of neo-liberal, turbo-capitalism has been an abysmal failure, based as it is on a theory and practice, out of sync with contemporary circumstances related to ecological and social justice. David Harvey sums up the 'bottom line', not the measurement of 'excessive profits' but of excessive suffering. " For those left or cast outside the market system – a vast reservoir of apparently disposable people bereft of social protections and supportive social structures – there is little to be expected from neoliberalization except poverty, hunger, disease' and despair." (D. Harvey, P. 185)

14 TRANSFORMATION IN CONSCIOUSNESS

The depth of this social and economic crisis has been recognised for a long time, explicitly and implicitly. A transformation in consciousness, motivation and political commitment is being reflected in diverse protests and movements across the world that have emerged to challenge neo-liberalism either head on or in ways that repudiate its logic and ideology. They include a 'sprawling environmental movement' with an assortment of green protests attempting to bind political action with ecological concerns; the building of LETS, (local economic trading systems), associations; the spread of religious groups, both formal and informal, preaching anti-market or anti-neo-liberal creeds; the joint activity of centre-left coalitions in Latin America being one of the most significant developments of our time. The continent that was raped, pillaged, terrorised and murdered has caught up with many of its key persecutors and put them on trial. But just as significant, new representative political and economic forms have surfaced, highlighting different approaches to market exchange and distribution; reinstating the ideal of public ownership, reinforced by anti- privatisation protests; cooperative and worker controlled, workplace experiments - shades of Jimmy Reid and UCS; creative ways of redistributing land, wealth and instituting social welfare programmes. Combining many of these developments has culminated in Venezuela's commitment to social and economic justice pursued by the charismatic Hugo Chavez and his successor on an agenda of '21st Century Socialism', backed by grass roots agitation and activity. " Despite the overwhelming cult of personality surrounding Chavez, and his moves to centralize power at the state level, the progressive 'networks' in Venezuela are at the same time highly decentralized, with power dispersed at the grass roots and community level, through thousands of neighbourhood councils and co-ops." (Naomi Klein, P. 573) The socialist ideals of Allende were driven into the psyche of a continent through Friedman's 'shock doctrine' and Pinochet generated fear. They are now resurrected by a resurgence of confidence in grass roots movements for radical change. " Ever since the Argentine collapse in 2001, opposition to privatization has become the defining issue of the continent, able to make governments and break them; by late 2006, it was practically creating a domino effect...." (Naomi Klein, P. 571)

In Latin American countries where political promises have not materialised, an erosion and cynicism regarding the democratic process has taken place. In Latin America, this is a positive response and helps to raise political awareness. Protests and mass movements for radical change are also in evidence in Europe, Russia, China and Asia. Perhaps the trial of 'key players' and reformist challenges to the neo-liberal juggernaut are minor by comparison but it cannot be denied that the 'neo-liberal creation myth' has been seriously undermined across the whole world. Before the emergence of these events, " The economic crusade managed to cling to a veneer of respectability and lawfulness as it progressed. Now that veneer was being very publicly stripped away to reveal a system of gross wealth inequalities, often opened up with the aid of grotesque criminality." (Naomi Klein, P. 564) But even more damning than this condemnation, these events have negated Friedman's association of 'freedom' with neo-liberal capitalism and President Bush's "... single sustainable model for national success: freedom, democracy and free enterprise." (Bush, Quoted in Naomi Klein, P. 565) The knowledge that Bush's declaration was backed up with overwhelming military might has not stopped the waves of protest – even in America against free market dogma.

Writing in 2005, David Harvey speculated about America's fate should an economic crash occur. Would, in fact, America grow its way out of its 'self-inflicted problems' or would the United States continue to live in a corporate fantasy world to be sharply awakened when, "....seemingly invulnerable entities like Enron came crashing down?" (David Harvey, P. 192) The US ruling elite might also think that it could, "....survive a global crisis in good shape..." but Harvey's greatest fear, in being aware of neo-liberal 'shock doctrine' tactics and strategies, was that the US, "In the wake of a financial crash, the ruling elite may hope to emerge even more empowered than before." (Harvey, P. 192) And with this empowerment would America show more of its darker side, a 'nationalism' of internal threats and fear for which it has established numerous, privatised institutions of national 'homeland' security? Externally, US nationalism and imperial power is expressed through, 'excessive and unilateralist interventionism' which, paradoxically, stems from America being more isolated, politically, culturally and militarily than ever before. " Externally, this nationalism leads to covert action and now to pre-emptive wars to eradicate anything that seems like the remotest threat to the hegemony of US values and the dominance of US interests." (Harvey, P. 196) And that covert action includes the suppression of both domestic and foreign dissent. The CIA supported coups against Chavez, Allende and other leaders of foreign countries – principally in Latin America - are prime examples of American 'covert' intervention in action. And if direct intervention is unacceptable to foreign states, then the sophisticated technology of 'drone' warfare can be deployed to minimise American casualties but maximise the breeding grounds of nationalist opposition, mainly Islamic, to United States foreign policy.

The above protests and movements express a myriad of ways to bring forth a new visionary world. They are novel ways of re-arranging our social, political, economic and cultural structures, both to enhance the quality of our lives and relationships and establish humane values and moral and ethical conduct. Although there is a recognition that common threads run through these movements and a World Social Forum is now in existence to express and define these 'commonalities', there does not appear to have emerged as yet, a general philosophy or vision to bind these commonalities into an organisational and political force capable of challenging the global power of neo-liberalism and promoting a fundamental social and cultural transformation. There is also the problem of the 'divide and rule' tactics of ruling elites, inter-ethnic violence fuelled by competing interests and the violent suppression of radical groups and movements. Focusing on local solutions and unaware of the common extent of similar problems on the macro scale also contributes to division and isolation.

According to Harvey, "Finding the organic link between these different movements is an urgent theoretical and practical task." (Harvey, P. 203) In practical terms, he sees 'uneven geographical development' as a major weakness in struggling to first constrain, then undermine and eventually replace global capitalism with more radical, social and democratic arrangements. However, by exposing the contradictions inherent in neo-liberal rhetoric and its anti-democratic monopolization and centralization of power it should be easier, Harvey argues, to appreciate that what lurks behind the utopian rhetorical mask is naked 'ruling-class power'. This power is not that of traditional class conflict, but the more subtle contemporary power of finance capitalism, criminal banking syndicates and corrupt corporations which can call upon colluding, political establishments, especially of the 'neo-con' variety in America and Conservative governments in Britain to provide sympathetic media space to right wing ideologues and demagogues to confuse and 'hoodwink' the people.

The political direction of New Labour in emulating Mrs Thatcher's policies and the Liberal party's present coalition arrangements with the Tories, highlights the movement of two centre-left parties to the centre-right of British, consensus politics. It is misleading to think that Thatcherism was born solely of Margaret Thatcher's conviction politics. She was certainly key to its devastating, socially engineered delivery, as was President Reagan in America. " Increasingly....the abrasiveness of neo-liberal ideologues made the Conservatives appear as the 'Nasty Party', at first leaving inner cities to rot unaided, later impoverishing the welfare dependent, and presiding apparently unconcerned over nationwide waves of riots in 1981, 1985 and 1990." (The Achievement of Thatcherism is that Britain Now Has Three Political Parties of the Right, Patrick Donleavy, Social Europe Journal, 25/04/2013) However, influenced by Hayek, in Britain and Friedman and the 'Chicago School' in America, Thatcher acted in unison with powerful right-wing players and financial power brokers to consolidated neo-liberal principles as the new economic inspiration and visionary aspiration for national and global hegemony. The theoretical gurus of free-market economics, with Thatcher, Blair and Brown, their willing political agents - like their counterparts across the world - have together led the world economy into the current financial quagmire while extolling the virtues of an ideology that contradicts and is incompatible with any serious efforts to save the planet. In this respect, "The era of neoliberalisation also happens to be the era of the fastest mass extinction of species in the Earth's recent history. If we are entering the danger zone of so transforming the global environment, particularly its climate, as to make the earth unfit for human habitation, then the further embrace of the neoliberal ethic and of neoliberalising practices will surely prove nothing short of deadly." (Harvey, P. 173)

To the ultimate detriment of democracy, the global economy has in effect been hijacked and diverted into the service of ever decreasing numbers of global corporations and financial institutions. Their vision, it would appear, is to relieve the capitalist system and its nefarious operations from any moral or ethical constraint and turn the world into a grand casino where 'spivs and speculators' write the balance sheets and determine who wins and who loses. All the economic statistics and graphs on income inequality across the world convincingly demonstrate this reality. To all accounts the recession has not weakened the determination of transnational corporations to weather the global economic storm. By utilising their well honed, evasive tax practices to salt away huge monetary resources, they are preparing for the next upsurge in growth and expansion.

It has been estimated that between them they control around twenty to thirty trillion dollars. (quoted by Peter Tatchell, MP, 'Question Time', programme, 23/05/2013) According to Robert Reich, "As global capital becomes ever more powerful, giant corporations are holding governments and citizens up for ransom....The fact is, global corporations have no allegiance to any country; their only objective is to make as much money as possible – and play off one country against another to keep their taxes down and subsidies up, thereby shifting more of the tax burden to ordinary people." (Robert Reich, Global Capital and the Nation State, Social Europe Journal, 20/05/2013) Cases in point include, Goldman Sachs negotiating a 'sweet heart' deal with the British Government over a tax dispute; Google – stated to be 'devious,calculating, and unethical' by the parliamentary chairman investigating the company's tax avoidance through its subsidiary in Ireland and Amazon, through its base in Luxembourg, "now receives more in subsidies from the British government than it pays here in taxes." (Robert Reich, Social Europe Journal, 20/05/2013)

These revelations all point to the fact that governments appear to be impotent in relation to the power of the modern corporation. Seeking international agreement through international bodies like the G. Eight, World Bank and IMF, whose history and policies have been tainted by association with corporate agendas, may be difficult, if not pointless. The fact that the corporations have been the most vociferous in their criticism of climate change and have poured vast sums of money into the Republican Party in order to challenge the scientific basis of environmental degradation perhaps illustrates that social and economic transformation has to come from the ground up. Nicholas Stern, who presented a report to the British Government on climate change in 2006, has said that he got it wrong. He recently reported that climate warming was not increasing by two to three degrees but by four degrees and if this trend continued, the planet would, eventually, be uninhabitable. (Informed by Andrew Watt, Social Europe Journal, 28/01/2013)

It is clear that global institutions and the European Union will only consider tweaking the relationship between multi-national corporations and governments over questions of tax avoidance, legalistic infringements and financial regulation. However, even tweaking frightens conservative governments who over the last three decades have built up London as one of the world's major financial centres. The fear of transaction taxes and other European regulation are the reasons behind their obdurate stance on Europe.

There is no evidence from European governments other than Nordic countries of any thorough going questioning of the debilitating role of the global 'cowboy economy'. This simply confirms the belief that for governments generally, radical alternatives are unthinkable. However, breaking links in the neo-liberal chain is possible. We have seen radical movements making real efforts to do this in Latin America. Is there then a possibility of countering neo-liberal ideology in Western 'democracies' and more specifically in an independent Scotland? Will Scotland, in its independence referendum, go with progressive social trends and create what the Scottish First Minister described as a 'very special society' and in the process shine like a beacon of light on an otherwise darkening economic and political horizon.

15 TOWARDS A JUST AND HUMANE WORLD

It would be a massive error of political judgement to see the present global crisis as just another cyclical hic-up, albeit more politically troublesome, in the long series of economic recessions thrown up by the contradictions in capitalism. Although acknowledged as the gravest recession since the 1929 crash, many 'progressive' economists appear to think that by adopting policies other than austerity programmes, the corroded engine of neo-liberal capitalism will spring back to life and the green shoots of growth will come again, like the American cavalry, to the rescue of Western economies. 'Disaster capitalism', in the form of unregulated financial centres, banks, and corporations along with compliant, inverted democratic states, is a devouring economic carnivore which has not only brought the economies of the West down, but has, over the last thirty years - mainly through American military hegemony and its myth-creating, neo-liberal ideology - inflicted economic destitution, murder and wars in Latin America and the Middle East. Oliver Stone's book reveals the undeniable effects of American imperial militarisation and its role in guaranteeing America's world wide economic interests, whatever the cost. It is a sobering thought that the United States is now 'beefing' up its military bases on the pacific coast of China, thus implying that China – because its economy is set to overtake America's in the near future - is the next 'enemy'. America is now faced with its Chinese nemesis, another powerful, abusive, corporate capitalist state, as greedy as itself, in the pursuit of unlimited economic growth while competing for the dwindling resources of the earth. Future conflict over these resources is inevitable if our current mindset continues.

The American system of government, has created an industrial-military complex that not only has an undue influence over it but is also heavily economically dependent on it for work and arms sales abroad. With its military might, the United States is evidently prepared to defend - to the death in some cases - an economic ideology that has enriched the one percent of the global establishment while economically crippling ninety nine percent of humanity. In order to support the privileges, wealth and power of the few - embedded in financial, banking and corporate institutions - over the hardship and destitution of the many, a 'war on terror' propaganda has been ramped up, along with its concomitant surveillance activities and abuse of human rights. This idea was spread throughout the Western world, particularly by Presidents Reagan, Bush and now Obama and the Republican neo-conservatives, whose fraudulent 'vision' is to dominate the world through America's ingrained belief in its own 'exceptionalism' and role as the world's 'overseer'.

Ian Macwhirter responded to the British government's claim that the UK is now emerging from the recession. He states that, "... we are experiencing a collective economic delusion arising from austerity fatigue and Government propaganda. Far from the economy turning a corner, it is running on empty." (Ian Macwhirter, Sunday Herald, 'Bust Britain..', 18/08/2013, P.8) The basis of this comment is the fact that 'household debt is running at 153% of GDP' (Ian Macwhirter) Most Western countries, are now either heavily in debt or bankrupt. While 'funny' money is being spewed out of Central Banks because the system has to be saved at the people's expense, is it an exaggeration to declare that most Western countries are now 'running on empty'? What this apt metaphor illustrates more than anything is that it is not only Western economies that are 'running on empty', but the governments and leaders of Western civilisation are running 'empty' of ideas and more seriously, running 'empty' of any 'vision' that seeks to put humanity on the road to a sustainable future. However, we should make no mistake, there is a global corporate 'vision' in place, blinkered as it may be. It is one in which the social, political and economic horizon stretches to an infinity of unlimited growth, acquisitive materialism and 'possessive individualism', bordering on a dogmatic belief that there can be no alternative economy or society beyond forms of predatory capitalism. The maintenance of an equilibrium between safeguarding the Earth while providing material and psychological security, egalitarian principles, compassion, contentment and happiness to the vast majority of humanity is a vision denied on the simple basis that it would never work in practice. Is this the meaning of 'realpolitic', the explanation used by politicians for doing nothing?

It is understandable, given human suffering, that during this recession, environmental and ecological concerns have been generally missing from governments agendas. It should not be a surprise that the cacophony of voices from economic think tanks, government departments and party leaders have been focused on growing the economy in order to crank up the industrial and manufacturing motor and get populations back to work – producing, selling and consuming. What ever economic system emerges after this recession or, hopefully, one with more vision for the future, populations will have to work to produce, sell and buy what is produced. But unlimited economic growth for its own sake will, inevitably, only complete another cycle of failure, especially as modern technology reduces the chance of satisfactory employment and quality of life, given the flexible nature of modern working practices, such as 'zero hours' contracts which are becoming ever more popular with employers. However, the catastrophic economic events and psychological traumas inflicted on the majority of people, together with a growing understanding of the contradictory flaws and myths in neo-liberal ideology, combined with the continuing corporate onslaught on the physical environment, are awakening the political consciousness of those who are suffering directly from this human constructed tragedy. Science has often come to the rescue of humanity with a host of discoveries, inventions and sometimes technological fixes. The quantum paradigm is one such discovery. Quantum physics sees further into cosmic reality than any other science to date and is now being emulated through new approaches and advances in other sciences which go beyond a mechanistic viewpoint. The life sciences are evolving paradigm shifts of their own and in turn are influencing the social sciences. Together they are moving towards a 'systems theory' and view of life which presents hope for humanity to evolve a better way of living. (Capra, The Web of Life).

The idealist 'vision' presented here is a deep ecological world view, which, hopefully will evolve, over a period time, from a 'human centred' focus to an 'earth centred' focus. As argued here, this is not intended to diminish humanity but to enhance humanity's integral place in the grand, universal scheme of things and help it to survive as a species. The awe inspiring discoveries of quantum mechanics has explicitly and implicitly demonstrated that humanity's fragmented existence and very survival is not only out of kilter with the natural world but out of kilter with our capacity to psychological and physically cope with the problems of modern society. For all practical purposes we are still transfixed with, and mentally and emotionally attached to, the Newtonian mechanistic paradigm, social Darwinism and its accompanying dysfunctional, competitive behaviour and materialistic values. The old paradigm is founded on a variety of assumptions which have evolved into ideas and values that have become entrenched in our modern mindsets. Among these assumptions are; in understanding the parts we can deduce the whole; our bodies are sophisticated machines; that society is a struggle for survival through aggressive competition; that scientific materialism holds the answer to everything; that unlimited growth through technological innovation is the way forward; that the patriarchal society is being overcome. All these assumptions have been radically challenged by the quantum paradigm and now found wanting, especially in practice where they have become inherently aberrant and destructive. This approach also challenges the assumption that the present environmental crisis is not caused by human intervention but is simply one of nature's cyclical rhythms. But even if that was the case we would still have to adapt our way of life to survive the vicissitudes of climate change and our dysfunctional social and economic arrangements. Is it therefore, an accident that these two interacting dynamic factors coming together bear no relation to each other? Most of the scientific evidence suggests otherwise, especially given the fact that the opposition is indirectly supported by massive corporation contributions and successive American governments who are generally reluctant to give climate change facts full credibility.

The quantum paradigm has discovered an integral harmony within the natural order that sees only integration, interconnectedness and interdependence. Here, Prince Louis De Broglie, a quantum physicist who defined genuine science as being motivated by spiritual ideals, explains what modern science is revealing, " As our attainments were freed from the mists in which they were first immersed, science took its modern form. Thus scientists have come to feel more and more keenly that there exists in nature an order, a harmony, which is at least partially accessible to our intelligence, and they have devoted all their efforts to discover each day more of the nature and the extent of this harmony." (Quoted from Physics and Microphysics, 1955, in Quantum Questions, Ed. By Kenneth Wilbur, 1984, P.115) Deep ecology acknowledges this harmony and has developed a theoretical conceptual foundation on which to further the integration of practical, sustainable solutions compatible with this natural harmony. Lester Brown of the Worldwatch Institute defines a 'sustainable' society as, "...one that satisfies its needs without diminishing the prospects of future generations." (Quoted in The Web of Life, F. Capra, P. 4) For humanity to create a sustainable society, given our present global predicament, requires a monumental transformational shift in our thinking, perceptions and social values. But as this book has tried to show, this 'quantum shift' has already begun.

The realisation that humanity is embedded in and dependent on the universal, 'cyclical processes of nature' gives deep ecology its apparent strength over 'shallow ecology'. Although the latter has achieved very good work in promoting a green agenda and making people more aware of the critical state of the earth's ecology, it is still anthropocentric in outlook, reducing nature to only an instrumental 'use' value. In contrast, deep ecology holds that humans are only a thread in the universal 'web of life' and as such cannot be given a superior place or priority in the matrix of Gaia, the ideal, ecologically intricate and interdependently balanced living system we inhabit. The complexity of this natural system has given rise to 'systems' thinking which endeavours to take account of all the interconnecting relationships in nature and through this broad scientific approach believes that, " Ultimately, deep ecological awareness is spiritual or religious awareness. When the concept of the human spirit is understood as the mode of consciousness in which the individual feels a sense of belonging, of connectedness, to the cosmos as a whole, it becomes clear that ecological awareness is spiritual in its deepest essence." (The Web of Life, F. Capra, P. 7)

The notion of 'spirit' makes an ecological consciousness consistent with the ancient 'perennial philosophy' and spiritual traditions of both East and West. Though these traditions are far distant from contemporary life in terms of science and technology, they are a vital product of our human evolutionary history. The quantum paradigm, it would appear, has taken humanity in an upwards spiral back to the natural world. This has given humans the opportunity and responsibility to raise their levels of awareness to once again bring humanity back into harmony with the natural order, rather than using our immense scientific and technological power to drive a destructive wedge between the two and threaten our survival as the most 'gifted', but most wayward species on earth.

Deep ecology is asking the deepest questions about our industrial culture, its unsustainable growth and materialist values. Despite many advances towards gender equality, Western and global society remains predominantly patriarchal. Eco-feminism is a major school within deep ecology and views,.." the patriarchal domination of women by men as the prototype of all domination and exploitation in the various hierarchical, milita-

113

ristic, capitalist, and industrial forms. They point out that the exploitation of nature, in particular, has gone hand in hand with that of women, who have been identified with nature throughout the ages. This ancient association of women and nature links women's history and the history of the environment, and is the source of a natural kinship between feminism and ecology." (The Web of Life, F. Capra, P. 9)

A transformation in human values runs parallel with a major shift in paradigms. Progressive values will emerge when our human tendency to self-assertiveness is balanced with an equal tendency towards our empathetic and integrative natures. The former tendency is largely linked to male domination. Excessive power is related to excessive self-assertion which is mostly found in social, economic and political hierarchies and any undermining of this power and the status and identity that goes with it often threatens and creates fear in those involved. But other forms of power are emerging in tune with the quantum paradigm which focuses on the idea of 'networks' rather than hierarchies and elites and has become ecology's 'central metaphor'. With this metaphor, a new ethics is being born which embraces all life forms. " It is a world view that acknowledges the inherent value of non-human life. All living beings are members of ecological communities bound together in a network of interdependencies. When this deep ecological perception becomes part of our daily awareness, a radically new system of ethics emerges." (The Web of Life, F. Capra, P. 11)

An eco-ethics of this kind will have a profound effect on the use and misuse of science and technology and their applications to human society and the natural world. Science is not value free as is often claimed. Our values filter through our perceptions and decisions, being influenced and shaped by the dominant paradigm in place at the time. The quantum paradigm has confirmed the principle of 'oneness' that exists behind the apparent divisions we see on the surface of our material world. Anchored on this notion it is not difficult to imagine an expansion of our awareness and consciousness that includes a harmony between the human 'self' and nature. The quantum paradigm is revealing the universal and cosmic oneness of nature. From that, the scientific framework for an ecological world view illustrates the potential humanity now has to construct a more just and egalitarian world in harmony with the natural order of all that exists.

The world has celebrated the 50th anniversary of Martin Luther King's, 'I have a dream' speech. If humanity is to survive the present global crisis then we shall all have to have a dream and act on it before it is too late. John Lennon was another 'dreamer' whose presence and sudden departure reflects both the possibilities and the challenges facing humanity at this critical point in time. His intuitive sense of retrieving hope from despair was expressed in the poetic words of his famous song 'Imagine'. 'You may say I'm a dreamer, but I'm not the only one. I hope some day you'll join us and the world will live as one.' Such 'dreams' and 'vision', if strived for and put into effect, would realise Jimmy Reid's clarion call for a 'creative re-orientation of society' and with it a cultural, social and, in his own words, a 'spiritual transformation' of society, the planet and all its people. His use of the word 'creative' suggests that what he had in mind was the simple application of our untrammelled imaginations to bring forth a humane world, worthy of being called human, compassionate and just.

REFERENCES

- Bohm, D., Wholeness and the Implicate Order, 1980
- Capra, F., The Turning Point: Science, Society and the Rising Culture, 1982.
- Capra, F., The Web of Life: A New Synthesis of Mind and Matter, 1996.
- Capra, F., The Tao of Physics: An exploration of the parallels between modern physics and Eastern mysticism, 1975.
- Cohen, D., Psychologists on Psychology, 1977.
- Fanon, F., The Wretched of the Earth, 1961
- Fisher, M., Capitalist Realism: Is There No Alternative
- From, E., The Anatomy of Human Destructiveness, 1973.
- Grof, S., Beyond the Brain, 1985.
- Harvey, D., A Brief History of Neo-liberalism, 2005
- Kasser, T., The High Price of Materialism, 2002.
- Keck, R., Sacred Eyes, 1992.
- Klein, N., The Shock Doctrine: The Rise of Disaster Capitalism, 2007.
- Krugman, P., End the Depression Now, 2012.
- Lansley, S., The Cost of Inequality, 2012
- Laslow, E., Quantum Shift in the Global Brain, 2008
- Latouche, S., Farewell to Growth, 2007.
- Lorimer, D., Whole in One, 1990.
- Macpherson, C., The Political Theory of Possessive Individualism:Hobbes to Locke. 1962
- Mason, P., Why Its Kicking Off Everywhere: The New Global Revolutions, 2012.
- Memmi, A., The Colonizer and the Colonized, 1965
- Nye, R., Three Views of Man, 1975
- Patel, R., The Value of Nothing: How to Reshape Market Society and Redefine Democracy, 2009.
- Peston, R., Who Runs Britain, 2008.

- Reid, J., The Glasgow Rectorial Address, 1972.
- Reid, J., Power Without Principles, 1999.
- Reid, R., The Concept of Radical Adult Education, with particular reference to Paulo Freire, Ivan Illich and the Third World, Manchester University, 1984.
- Sheldrake, R., The Science Delusion: Freeing the Spirit of Enquiry, 2012.
- Sheldrake, R., The Rebirth of Nature, 1990
- Schumacher, E., Small Is Beautiful, 1973.
- Social Europe Journal.
- Scottish Left Review.
- Stone O., Kuznick P., The Untold History Of The United States, 2012
- Wilbur, K., Quantum Questions: Mystical Writings of the World's Great Physicists, 1984.
- Wilbur, K., Up From Eden: A Transpersonal View of Human Evolution, 1981.
- Wilbur, K., Spectrum of Consciousness, 1977.
- Wolin, S., Democracy Incorporated: Managed Democracy and the Specter of Inverted Totalitarianism, 2008.
- Zohar, D., Marshall, I., The Quantum Society: Mind, Physics and a New Social Vision, 1993.
- Zohar, D., The Quantum Self, 1991.

ABOUT THE AUTHOR

Robert Reid is a retired teacher. He was educated at Aberdeen University where he studied history. He went on to gain a Master's degree in Adult Education and Community Development at Manchester University. He has a keen interest in social and cultural history, in particular the transformative power of emerging scientific paradigms and their influence on shaping and conditioning predominant values, attitudes, belief systems and personal and collective behaviour.

6680931R00071

Printed in Great Britain
by Amazon.co.uk, Ltd.,
Marston Gate.